I0618829

An Heir for the Secret Prince

An Aldonia Royals Novel

Kristine Lynn

The characters and events in this book are fictitious. Any similarity to real persons, living or dead, places, or events is coincidental and not intended by the author.

If you purchase this book without a cover you should be aware that this book may have been stolen property and reported as "unsold and destroyed" to the publisher. In such case the author has not received any payment for this "stripped book."

An Heir for the Secret Prince
An Aldonia Royals Novel #1
Copyright © 2021 Kristine Lynn
All rights reserved.

ISBN: (ebook) 978-1-7373794-0-9
(print) 978-1-7373794-1-6

Inkspell Publishing
207 Moonglow Circle #101
Murrells Inlet, SC 29576

Cover art by: Fantasia Frog Designs
Edited by: Audrey Bobek

This book, or parts thereof, may not be reproduced in any form without permission. The copying, scanning, uploading, and distribution of this book via the internet or via any other means without the permission of the publisher is illegal and punishable by law. Please purchase only authorized electronic or print editions, and do not participate in or encourage piracy of copyrighted materials. Your support of the author's rights is appreciated.

To Shawn, my real-life prince. Our story is just beginning.

KRISTINE LYNN

CHAPTER ONE: THE ROYAL ADVISOR

Aurelia bit her bottom lip and scowled at the man in front of her. She was both pleasantly surprised and disappointed to discover that the Prince was *everything* she thought he'd be.

Hot as melted sin on a cracker.

Obviously a player.

Richer than most countries.

Seemingly perfect. *Ugh.*

With wavy, blond hair, perfectly straight, white teeth, and a tanned body that looked like he was familiar with a gym, he was precisely what her overactive imagination had drummed up on the three flights it had taken her to arrive in Aldonia. *A royal hunk.* Not to mention, he seemed to have a decent sense of humor and treated the servers who flitted in and out of the open-air courtyard with respect, bordering on deference.

She dug around the depths of her purse, a bag big enough to hold all the tools she might need for an interview like this. She felt like Mary-freaking-Poppins as she shifted through more ChapSticks than a single woman should have in one space, a few snacks left over from the plane, and some feminine products she thought she'd left in her luggage until she found what she was looking for.

Her lifeline: her cell phone.

Flipping right to her contacts, she scrawled a hasty text message to her best friend, Lily, keeping tabs on the Prince out of the corner of her eye. He navigated the regal space with ease, a new scantily clad woman on his arm each time he passed. Typical. A chuckle devoid of humor bubbled up from her chest.

Briefly, she considered the time difference between Aldonia and New York before she hit send. Three a.m. on a Friday night? No chance Lily was asleep, not when her job as a party planner literally demanded otherwise. She shot it off without another thought.

Bad news. Prince is cute—you'd even say hot—and seems nice enough. Funny, even. Boo. :(

Aurelia swirled her merlot around her tongue while she paced the marble floors of the grand courtyard. Wow, even the wine was superb. But of course it was. Royalty could afford actual champagne taste. One of the perks.

Speaking of perks, Aurelia let her gaze wander from the Prince to the palace, another story altogether when it came to opulence. She took in each detail, committing it to memory so she could share it with Lily and her father when she got home. The light from the chandeliers draping the walls in glittering detail that looked almost organic. The walls reverberating the cacophony of conversations in muted echoes that filled the cavernous space. The accents that floated by her resonated with culture and finesse, each one like a fingerprint, as different as the next.

Only Aurelia stood out, no accent to speak of, save the long vowels of an east coaster, a rented dress with a hem an inch too long for her petite frame, and hair and makeup done by the only stylist she knew—herself. A severe case of imposter syndrome crept up her spine now that she was surrounded by so much royalty and grandeur.

As long as she could, as her father so aptly put it, fake it until she made it, she'd be fine. She inhaled deeply, the creosote from the desert outside the palace tickling her nose.

When her phone buzzed in her hand, Aurelia peeked at it through the heavy fake lashes Lily insisted were stylish this season. Yeah, if she liked the idea of adding half a pound to each eyelid. This was officially the last time she listened to Lily about anything fashion related. Her ankles still hadn't recovered from her best friend's knee-high, leather boot advice on her last assignment in Milan.

Am I supposed to feel bad that you have to spend the week with a royal hunk? What's the prob? Call me when you have something actually interesting to report. Send pics pls! Xoxo

Well, that was the problem, wasn't it? Aurelia could neither send a photo to Lily, nor did she have anything interesting to report, other than the classy ostentatiousness of the palace. It meant she'd likely wasted her time and money by flying halfway around the world to write about a down-to-earth royal who, at least from what she could see on the surface, had nothing interesting lurking beneath.

He was normal, boring even, and neither sold copies.

Ugh.

How was she ever supposed to become an award-winning journalist if she kept landing lackluster stories? *Knock it off*, she told herself. *It's up to you to find the story, not wait for it to fall in your lap.*

So, she would. She'd find a story if she had to make one herself. If she didn't... Well, she didn't want to think about that right now. It was time to concentrate, prove she had a right to be there as much as anyone else, rented dress and shoes be damned. Her mother's voice whispered from a safe, tucked away place in her subconscious.

Be patient, love. You know what you're doing. Just take your time and listen.

Aurelia shut her eyes against the sting that came with the whisper. Her mom would have been right, though. Aurelia had come to Aldonia with only an idea and a tip. She had to suss out the rest herself.

With each sip of as close to perfect wine as she'd ever had, she catalogued what she knew about the Prince that she might be able to spin in her article.

No one had ever been able to capture a photo of him, nor his family in all the years they'd reigned. Odd, yes, but not story-worthy on its own.

She needed more.

He also apparently had an advisor who'd started as a friend of the family. Some secret encounter had led to the guy landing the royal gig, but no one had seen a picture of him, either.

Mysterious, but still not Pulitzer-winning.

Third, and arguably most important, the Prince was second in line to the throne of Aldonia, not to mention about a billion and a half American dollars, making the unphotographed Prince Gregory one of the wealthiest men on the planet. Again, nothing the world didn't already know. Though it might explain why women threw themselves at his feet—not to mention in his bed—at their first glimpse of the man. The half-chuckle made its way up her throat again.

She wasn't so naïve that she didn't understand money and appearance were all that mattered in some circles. It just didn't in hers. Money hadn't ever impressed her, but honestly, neither had a handsome face; both were traits a person was born into. Neither said anything about their character. Her ex-husband, Brian, had both, and look how that had turned out. She rubbed the scar at the base of her skull absently.

The ten or so women hanging all over the Prince clearly didn't share that sentiment. Their canned lines dripped with desperation, and they pawed at him in dresses hiked up enough to show everything God gave them. It would be tacky if it weren't so entertaining.

Aurelia fought yet another bubble of laughter that pressed against her chest. Maybe they didn't see the "formal dress" part of the invitation to the party. Or so she hoped.

The truth was, Aurelia didn't care in the least about Prince Gregory or his fortune. He was a story, plain and simple. A means to an end that came with a week abroad on assignment in a place that served dang good wine and hors d'oeuvres.

When one of the women cackled, a high-pitched sound not unlike the hyenas from *The Lion King*, Aurelia let the giggle escape. It was louder than the noise from the idle conversations, and a few heads turned to look at her.

"Ms. Beck?"

Aurelia choked on her wine as she spun around to face the owner of the deep, sexy voice behind her, sloshing a good deal of what was left in her glass on his shoes in the process. Her heels caught on the long hem of her dress and she nearly toppled over.

Instead, strong hands wrapped around her, locking her in place. Her hand not holding the crystal stemware was pressed against a solid wall of muscled flesh, steadying herself.

"Crap," she muttered, looking down at the shiny black loafers that now had a third of her Merlot on them, patting the chest of the man who'd saved her from eating concrete. "I'm terribly sorry. I was waiting to speak with," she started, her arm flailing behind her in an errant attempt to point out the Prince, but her words—usually her specialty—stuck in her throat.

There, in front of her, his hands still gripping her bare arms, was the most breathtakingly beautiful man she'd ever seen.

Goosebumps erupted over her skin and heat flushed her cheeks.

Good God above.

All the air seemed sucked from the room, leaving her breathless and dizzy.

He was tall, so much so that her neck strained to look into his cerulean eyes. They were a pale blue-green, but *dark* was the first word that came to her, probably because of the cutting gaze directed at her.

She should probably do something about cleaning up his shoes that cost more than a month's rent of her apartment, but she couldn't look away. Besides, he seemed in no big rush to step back, give her an inch to breathe, take in the situation.

And was it ever a situation.

Every inch of her body—from her eyes that couldn't tear themselves from his gaze, to her feet that were starting to cramp in her peep-toe heels—was a tangle of nerves. His hair—too dark to fit in this desert world of sun-kissed manes—was short on the sides, long on top, and perfectly manicured. Her hands ached to brush through the strands that sat meticulously in place, to muss up his perfection just a bit so she didn't feel so out of place, so vulnerable all of a sudden.

When he released her, the skin beneath his grip blazed with electricity.

She shivered despite the heat that blew in from the desert outside the palace.

"You were saying?" he asked. His lips—*full, red, luscious,* her subconscious drummed up in the way of description— were pulled up in the corners in a wicked smile that seemed to mock her discomfort. She considered them more than the question he posed.

What might it be like to put those lips to hers?

She shook her head free of that thought, tempting as it was. The reason she was there, in a castle in the Middle East, won over the symphony of noise that urged her not-so-subtly to touch this stranger. Have him touch her.

Whoa. She shook her head more violently this time,

trying to erase the image for good. It didn't help that whoever this guy was, he was staring at her with amusement etched in his icy features. This was *so* not funny, and the fact that he thought it was didn't sit him in high regard with her. Arrogance wafted off him in waves.

But enough about him. What had come over *her*? Who cared that it had been more than a hot minute since she'd slept with a man? This was most definitely neither the time nor the place. Though when his broad hand rested on her shoulder and gave it a squeeze, she gulped back a wave of desire that argued otherwise.

She shrugged her shoulders back, shaking her bare skin free of his hand. It tingled where he'd touched her, branded her. She'd seen handsome men before, more than her fair share. The Prince himself could even fall under that category. Heck, the Prince was, as she'd texted Lily, hot. Not to mention available, nice as far as she could tell, and apparently hilarious judging by the cackles she heard from behind her. But she felt nothing for him.

So, why was she letting this stranger get the best of her now?

Come on, be professional. You need this.

And she did. This job, this story, was her only chance to get out from under the debt Brian left her with. She couldn't ask her father to help her anymore. Not after… Not after… She couldn't finish the thought without a lump forming in her throat. She swallowed it, along with her growing frustration at the stranger in front of her.

"Yes, I was. I'm waiting to speak with Prince Gregory." She jutted her chin out toward him, crossed her arms over her chest in sheer defiance of him, of what he did to her.

"You're a journalist."

Aurelia rolled her eyes. *Well, duh.* "Does the press pass around my neck give it away?" she shot back. That her voice didn't quiver like her insides she considered a major win.

His gaze traveled down from hers, pausing at the deep

V of her floor-length gown where her breasts peeked up from the satin. His gaze never made it to where the pass hung around her stomach, but his smile—the sinister one that made him look like he was up to no good—was back. Flames ignited just under her skin, starting in her cheeks and working their way south, consuming everything, including her good sense.

"And who might you be?" she finally got out.

Christ. Everything about this man made her crazy— and not all of it in the I-want-to-strangle-you way. She wasn't entirely sure she could blame the dampness trickling down her neck on the desert heat.

"No one of importance. One of the Prince's advisors, that's all."

At that, something clicked.

His posture, like that of a Greek god come to life. The glint in his eyes that spoke of experience. His solid-as-stone body that belied a rugged physicality.

She knew who he was.

"You're him. The advisor who saved his life or something like that, right?"

He smiled, showing off his set of straight, bone-white teeth, and heat settled in her stomach.

That grin. It made her damp in other areas as well. It was infuriating. *He* was infuriating. She didn't care who he was or what he'd done. The last thing she needed was a distraction that got in the way of what would be a difficult assignment either way.

"Something like that. I'm here to bring you to the royal chambers. The interview? Or had you forgotten?"

Had she forgotten? Did this advisor really think so much of himself that he imagined all her professionalism would fly the coop with his smile, seductive as it was? She'd be insulted if she weren't furious.

"I hadn't forgotten," she huffed, her chest straining under her efforts to keep her standing tall, proud. Though, now that she gave it some actual thought, she couldn't recall a single reason to see the Prince again, not when all her questions now focused on this man with eyes that seemed poised to kill. *Get it together.* "Forgive me for saying as much, but I'm not sure I'm comfortable being alone with the Prince in his private bedroom."

"You won't be alone. I'll be there, along with members of his private guard. That's for your safety as much as his, Ms. Beck."

"I didn't mean to imply…" she began, her cheeks growing hot to the touch again. Why did her body have to betray her at every turn by being so freaking transparent? And around him, no less. She needed to muster the same confidence the advisor had if she was going to keep up with him. With half the arrogance, of course.

"No need to apologize. Our Prince is a good man at heart." Something about the way his gaze traveled down her body seemed like an appraisal, like every word she spoke was a check in a column he judged. Was she passing his test? "But he has earned his reputation."

He turned with military precision and marched off in the other direction, leaving her standing alone near the fountain in the middle of the courtyard, wine glass near empty. She downed the last few sips in one gulp.

"Okay, I guess I'll follow you," she muttered, placing the goblet on a serving tray as a member of staff passed. Breathless and pissed at being so easily dismissed, she managed to catch up to him, and in strappy heels, no less. Sometimes she wished women got credit for doing everything men did—sometimes better—all in heels-from-Hell.

"Excuse me," she called out, tapping him on the shoulder and barely keeping her footing in the process. When he didn't turn around, she yelled louder, her voice echoing down the stone hallway. "Hey! Stop. *Please.*"

He did, and she almost ran smack into him, something she hoped not to make a regular occurrence.

He faced her, his arms crossed and hands resting on

biceps that threatened to cut through the fabric surrounding them. She struggled to keep from staring at his body, the one part of him she worried would thwart her resolve to do what she'd come to Aldonia to do.

"Yes?" he asked. Ooh, she could curse him for being miraculously unperturbed by the brisk walk and her obvious frustration. Her fingers itched to slap the smug smile right off his face.

"What's your name?" she asked, struggling to take in the dry, desert air with the unintended cardio.

"Philip. Though you may address me as 'Sir Philip.'"

"Oh, *may* I?"

His face remained as stoic as a marble statue. If he caught her sarcasm, he wasn't going to let her have the satisfaction; yet another frustrating trait about this man. They were beginning to stack up. "Isn't that what they call a knight in royal circles?"

"You do your research. I'm impressed. I was knighted by the Prince when I saved his life a few years back. Or something like that." The corners of his mouth turned up, the smile unnerving in its lack of humor.

"Of course, I do my research, *sir*." She enunciated the last word, hoping to rile him up the same way he got under her skin, but if he was fazed, he gave no indication. Smug bastard. "Research is part of my job," she added, feeling stupid as soon as the words were out of her mouth. Of course, it was, and of course he would know that. He probably dealt with the press every day on behalf of the Prince.

"Why aren't you here to do a story on the King? You know he and *his wife* are expecting next month."

Aurelia stopped in her tracks, noting the way Philip growled the words *his wife*. She needed a moment to collect why the words sounded different. Dangerous, even. She couldn't escape the *ping, ping, ping* of red flags assaulting her subconscious. Her editor at the small magazine she contracted with once told her she had extraordinary instincts for someone new to the gig, but to her, they were a necessity. Without them, who knew what Brian might have been capable of? If it came as an ancillary benefit now, then so be it. She just didn't know what to do next. How to proceed without scaring Philip off.

"This, uh, this is stunning." She pointed to a lone piece of art adorning the wall, a cryptic piece she recognized from her painting hobby.

"Thank you. It was expensive, so it should be. Shall we?" He waved her on, but she stalled, considering his dismissal of the King by way of his wife.

"Did the King purchase it?" she asked, trying for nonchalance. She was pleased when her voice came out even, steady.

"No. The Queen did. Years ago."

The tone he used to talk about the Queen sent chills racing down Aurelia's spine. The one thing she'd learned early was that her spine-tingling feelings were usually more telling than the words people said—she just had to know what to do about them.

This particular situation was tricky since she was dealing with royalty. Behaving like a thirsty hound wasn't going to win her any favors. Time to act like the award-winning journalist she wanted to be.

"Is it a Kandinsky?" she asked. Her question seemed to crack the advisor's imperturbable veneer. He smiled, this time with mirth. It was a good look on him. She almost told him as much, adding that he should wear it more often.

"It is. Good eye. Are you a collector?"

She laughed, a single bark that echoed down the corridor. "Not on my salary. Someday, hopefully. When I win a Pulitzer."

"Ambitious," he said, eyeing her carefully.

"Passionate."

"Hmmm. You still didn't answer my question."

"Typically, it's me asking them, not answering them."

"Do you always get what you want?" he asked her, crossing his arms over his broad chest. His eyes narrowed, appraising her with his sea-green, icy gaze that, like the rest of the man, seemed out of place in the desert palace.

"If I'm right, which I am. I was invited by the royal family to do an interview about the Prince, so that's what I'll do. Deal with it." She wished she could curb the defiance in her voice, but this man sent her emotions spiraling. Steadying her pulse around him was taking all the strength she had.

"I see. Well, let me make sure the Prince still has the time to speak with you," he said curtly, his brows pulled tight. "Wait here, please, Ms. Beck." He strode off in the direction of the party.

She'd crossed a line. What she didn't get was why this man made it so easy to react with knee-jerk responses, why she couldn't keep her composure around him. She needed to check her baggage at the door if she didn't want to walk out of there empty-handed in less than a week.

She closed her eyes tight, took a deep breath that was thick with the aroma of desert life beyond the walls. It reminded her of the time her mother had taken her on a road trip to Arizona in the summer when her dad got a part-time teaching gig at their local university. The monsoons had claimed the road they needed to take out of a small town south of Phoenix, but Aurelia hadn't minded at all. The smell of moisture in the desert, like life beginning again, had stayed with her the rest of the trip. Her mother would have loved it here in Aldonia. Aurelia put her hand to her heart, stilling the ache that thumped against her chest like an anvil being swung by a giant. She opened her eyes that had grown damp.

"Hold on," she called after Philip, surprised he hadn't gone as far as she thought. Like it or not, she needed this man to do her job.

When he stopped, she appreciated how each muscle in his shoulders strained against his dress shirt. He was built like a member of the guard, not an advisor. Questions she'd ask if he were her interviewee clogged the back of her throat.

Why had he been in the position of saving the Prince's life?

Where were the guards then?

What kind of advising did he do for the Prince?

None of it added up, nor had anything come up about Philip in her research except rumor and hearsay—not the type of solid ground she could build a story on. She didn't have all the pieces to try and make it fit, so she'd just have to be patient.

Not her strong suit. Her mother's voice came in the form of a small chuckle at that admission.

"I'm sorry. I'm interested in the Prince because he's interesting." A lie, especially with this enigma of a man standing next to her. "There aren't any photos of him circulating with any women despite his, as you call it, *reputation*, and we're in the age of social media. Surely at least one of the women he's, ahem, *dated*, got ambitious and managed a selfie at some point. But there's nothing. Nada. Zilch."

There was that smile again. The one that snuck past her defenses and made her wish he'd stop acting so surly and start using his lips for other things she was certain she'd enjoy more. When his arms crossed his chest, Aurelia gulped back a wave of lust. Each of his muscles looked functional, used frequently, none of them tamed with lethargy. He took a step toward Aurelia, and she caught the scent of mint mingled with something stronger, more organic. Like life in the desert.

It made her dizzy, among other things.

"The Prince doesn't allow phones or cameras in his company." Another step in her direction.

She stared up at him now, close enough to notice the stubble forming on his chin. He hadn't shaved that day— an oversight or something else? He was as much a mystery as the man he served.

Maybe more so.

Professional curiosity took a backseat to wishing she knew what the thick, short hairs would feel like against the bare skin of her chest and she shuddered. Christ, this man was danger incarnate. She needed to use him to get to the Prince, then steer clear of him at all costs.

"Why not? He's a public figure. Surely, he isn't that shy. All evidence otherwise seems to contradict that."

"True. Maybe he just doesn't want a bunch of pictures highlighting his mistakes."

His breath warmed her cheek, more intoxicating than the wine she'd shot in an attempt to chase him down.

This time, Aurelia moved toward him. She resisted the thrilling urge to place a palm on his chest, to feel the heat and hardness rather than just imagine it. Knowledge was definitely not power at that moment, as she remembered what the strength had felt like under her palm.

"Maybe he should stop making those mistakes."

Philip laughed, a guffaw that seemed to fill the narrow hallway they were still standing in. She wouldn't have been as surprised if he brought out a pet tiger as she was at the humor he'd reserved until then.

Taking a deep breath, he nodded.

"You should tell him that. God knows I've tried, and he doesn't listen to me. Maybe you'll make more headway."

Um, no. Aurelia shrunk back, her brow furrowed and lips pursed. She shook her head. "Not likely. Nice try, though."

Philip laughed again, softer this time, and took her hand. Sparks emanated from her palm when it met Philip's skin. The way he tensed, he must have felt the electric charge as well. But how did he feel about it?

"Do you have questions prepared?" he asked, his voice thicker than before. It shot straight to Aurelia's heart, then moved south to where moisture built between her thighs.

She shook her head. "Not really. Just some basic follow-up to my research." Why had she lied? She had a few hard-hitting questions about some rumors she'd dug up, many of them far from basic follow-up.

One such rumor was that the Prince was in love, engaged to be married, and the bride had left him for someone else. A very back-alley version of that rumor was that she left him for his brother, the King. It wouldn't surprise Aurelia any, especially the way she'd seen beautiful, young, curvy women throwing themselves at the Prince, who came with a title and fortune. An ambitious woman might not want to settle for a mere prince when she could have a king, a country.

Still, it would be a cruel rumor if it were true.

She needed to find that out tonight. It would be enough to save her story if she could quote the Prince admitting to the rumors it had taken her hours of research to dig up and combine that with Philip's disgust with the Queen. Maybe this assignment wouldn't be a waste of time. Maybe, just maybe, she'd pull this off.

Hope flooded her system.

"I have a feeling you'll think of something," he told her, his lips dangerously close to her ear. The sincerity in his voice unarmed her.

Philip took her through an ornately carved set of heavy wooden doors that moaned as if they were living creatures when he pushed through them. This castle—modest compared to the photos she'd seen of the King's palace in the capital of Aldonia—really was a work of art. Whatever flash judgments she'd passed about the Prince, she had to admit he had exquisite taste. It was lavish but reserved. Every bit of the art and décor seemed to serve a purpose, not unlike the advisor.

When Aurelia's eyes adjusted to the dimly lit room, she gasped. It was perfect, like something she'd dreamt up.

Exotic.

Regal.

Intimate.

Candles served as the only light in the room, but they were hidden behind gold lanterns with geometric cutouts, leaving the walls littered with triangles, stars, hexagons, and diamonds made of light. A tapestry adorned with an elephant mother and her baby hung where a headboard should be, but the frame of the bed looked organically connected to it. The carved oak posts bore the same intricate features as the door they'd just come through.

She'd never seen such ornate carvings, nor such perfectly suited furniture for a room. It threatened to take her breath away. As did the rest of the room when she shifted her attention outward.

The barrier in front of her was no more than a thin, satin curtain that blew open with the breeze, flaunting an impressive stone patio beyond the bedroom. Gold-rimmed water glasses and silverware sat on a table large enough for her to lie down on just before the exit to the patio, wine goblets filled beside each setting.

Between the dark wood and the lack of light, the room should have felt small, but casting a furtive glance at Philip and noting how small his overpowering frame appeared, she might have been standing in the middle of a field for how open it was. She'd most likely be conducting her interview there, making this the most stunning and exotic locale she'd ever worked. Nerves fluttered against her chest like butterflies trying to escape.

"Have a seat," Philip said, motioning to the table as she'd guessed. "The Prince will be here in a moment."

She nodded and obliged. The regality of the castle worked its magic on her more than when she'd arrived. She'd come expecting the sports cars, dresses, and jewelry to match the expensive taste of a foreign royal, but only the first part of that equation had rung true. Everything else showed restraint, class. Somehow, this was more intimidating than flaunting their innumerous wealth would have been.

The doors creaked opened and Prince Gregory waltzed in, flanked by two guards on each side. He laughed as he slugged a guard on the shoulder, drawing an exasperated sigh from Philip.

Interesting. Philip all but chastised the playful royal. Why? And what gave him the right? The now-familiar *ping, ping* of warning pelted her subconscious. The questions she had for Philip were starting to outweigh those she had for the Prince.

She stood, dipped her head toward him.

"Prince Gregory," she said, extending her hand toward him. "It's a pleasure to meet you. Thank you for agreeing to an interview; I know your time is valuable."

He left his hand entwined in hers, his eyes sparkling with mischief, so she panicked and reacted with the same generic move she'd seen in every rom-com since she was a preteen—she kissed the top of his hand.

He gasped in surprise, and Aurelia could swear she heard Philip stifle a laugh.

Oh, crap. No more taking cues from Netflix. Great start, Aurelia. The imposter syndrome that had ebbed in the past half hour flared again, almost overriding the warning bells.

Finally, after the longest pause Aurelia had ever suffered through, Prince Gregory laughed, clapping her on the shoulder, a gentler version of what he'd done with the guard.

"Yes. Well, aren't you a sight for sore eyes? An American, yes?"

Aurelia sighed with relief. She hadn't totally blown it. Still, she shoved her shoulders back, stood as tall as she could make her five-two frame appear. At least her stilettos helped. She needed to scrape together some semblance of dignity if she was going to come back from the silly kissing faux pas and establish herself as a professional to be taken seriously.

"I am. New Yorker, born and raised."

"Ah, I've always considered that city to be a foreign

country itself. I'm more of an open field, cowboy kinda guy, but New York is beautiful."

She looked at the Prince and saw a smart, but humble man. Her instincts were rarely wrong when it came to people. Still, something was off; she just couldn't place her finger on what, exactly.

"Have you been, then?"

"My sister," he started, then shot Philip a glance and stopped himself, "well, a woman I consider to be my sister, is studying there now. Her master's in Equine Management."

There were the tingles down her spine again. Warning bells rang loud in her mind, no longer a pinging but a full-fledged hurricane warning system on full alert. She just hadn't a clue why. She forced her mind to pay more attention to each word the Prince uttered, as well as those he didn't. It didn't help that somewhere behind her stood Philip, watching their whole exchange. Her body reacted to this knowledge viscerally, sending chills down her bare skin whenever the advisor coughed or shifted against the wall.

"Good for her. NYU?" she asked, turning her full attention back to the Prince.

"Columbia."

"Wow. Impressive."

"Thank you. Shall we sit?"

Aurelia nodded, cleared her throat, and reached for the bag she brought. The way the Prince talked about the woman in New York, they were either relatives or romantic feelings were involved. Since he'd said she was like his sister, though, the latter couldn't be true. She'd put that in her notes to review later since her research suggested he didn't have any female relatives other than his mother and sister-in-law. At least the questions now steered her toward her original story, not Philip. That didn't mean the advisor didn't stir up an array of queries that had nothing to do with her interview.

"May I use my phone to record the interview? I'm well aware of your policies surrounding photos, and assure you I will not break them."

He exhaled slowly, his brow furrowed as he considered her request. His playful smile returned after a few seconds. He was unabashedly handsome, and while she could see his appeal with females the more time she spent with him, she might as well have been his sister for all the attraction she felt.

"Against my better judgment, I'll allow it. But if you don't mind, my advisor, Philip, will check your phone before you leave."

Aurelia tried not to think about why a bolt of heat shot from the pit of her stomach to the arches of her feet when Prince Gregory mentioned Philip.

"Of course, Your Grace. I, um, brought my portfolio if you'd like to see it." She swallowed back the lust that the mere mention of the advisor sent racing through her veins. At least she'd successfully changed the subject.

"I'm sorry to ask you to bring them. It's a mere formality since we already saw most of it in the emails. We just need copies here at the palace."

"Of course."

She took a thin folder out of her bag and handed it over. The Prince thumbed through each piece thoughtfully, a smile on his face.

"This one is my favorite," he told her, pointing to a photo accompanied by a short blurb beneath it.

It was one of her first pieces, the only one she'd attempted to photograph herself. The story was a simple slice-of-life piece, but the photo, no, the photo captured her subject more than words ever could have. She'd been interviewing an older woman who had helped transport Jews across the border in Germany. The woman had lost her husband, her daughter, her job as a seamstress, the heavy losses evidenced in the deep creases surrounding her eyes. But the light reflected in the irises, the hint of a smile on the woman's face, belied a resilience Aurelia was jealous of. If only she could muster the inner strength to face her own demons like the woman had. It was inspiring.

"If only we allowed photographs. You have quite a gift. Your parents must be proud." Behind them, Philip coughed loudly. Gregory frowned and slipped the photo back in the folder in front of him.

"Thank you. My father is." Aurelia's cheeks burned with the unexpected praise. "Um, shall we begin?"

"Absolutely. But only if you have a drink with me. It's not often I get the chance to have a beautiful, American woman ask me questions other than about my money."

He lifted his glass and took a long sip of the deep red wine, and she laughed. She liked the Prince, found it easy to settle into comfort with him, though the bells alerting her that something didn't add up still rang in her subconscious.

Patience, her mother's voice reminded her.

"That's an easy sell." She pressed *record* on her phone, set it down on the table. "Well, you know I've got to start with the obvious question. What's with the *Puruse* attached to your name?" She looked at her notebook app on her phone. "Duke of Puruse, Prince of Aldonia? No one in America knew your given name was Gregory, and I can't find your birth name anywhere online, either. It's all very mysterious." She tossed him an easy smile, enjoying the playful banter with an interviewee for a change. She hadn't had much experience working with celebrities, and certainly no royalty before the Prince, but she hadn't expected this degree of pleasantness.

It was almost too easy to talk to him.

He put his pinky finger up to pursed lips like Mike Myers's character in *Austin Powers*, and she laughed.

"I assure you, it's anything but mysterious. Though I'm not sure I want to tell you the truth since it's actually rather dull."

She glanced sideways at him, crossed her arms over her

chest, tapping her biceps as if to imply she was impatiently waiting.

"Fine. You're a real, how do you say it in America? Ballbuster?" He laughed. "The name we are given at birth is irrelevant to our titles that show who and what we serve. I bear the title Duke of Puruse because this region is my foremost responsibility, one I was born into. However, if something happens to me, another Duke of Puruse, Prince of Aldonia will be given the title. It isn't important who they were before that."

"That's not as dull as you say it is. I'm fascinated. So, it sort of eliminates a *Game of Thrones* power struggle if anything were to happen to you."

"Precisely. I like a sharp-witted woman. As well as one who watches good television."

Aurelia laughed. She couldn't remember the last time she'd been unabashedly flirted with, but darn if it didn't feel good.

She cast a quick glance at Philip, who stood resolute against the wall, taking the same stance as the four guards. Any hint of his smug satisfaction at her hand-kissing slipup was gone. In fact, he looked more than a little annoyed at her, his green eyes narrow slits that resembled a cat on the hunt when he glanced in her direction. What had she done this time? And why was he still there with the guard? It seemed a bit redundant. Somehow, again, more questions than answers surfaced with Philip, an annoying trend she saw continuing as long as she was there.

Maybe he'd been a member of the guard in the past but had proven himself to be more valuable to the Prince. Either way, the man was more than he seemed to be, which was more than she could say for the transparent Prince who sat back in his chair, his feet up on the table, a glass of wine lazily resting in one hand.

As she launched into her prepared questions, the moody advisor behind her and out of view, she couldn't shake the feeling that she was interviewing the wrong person.

CHAPTER TWO: THE ROYAL OFFER

Philip's shoulders tensed as Aurelia fired question after question at Gregory. She was different from the rest. More dangerous. Something about her inquiries told him she took herself both more and less seriously than her predecessors who wrote bland reports on the royal family, afraid to rustle any feathers. Aurelia was precise like a surgeon, each question like a scalpel, designed to cut through the fluff to the meat. If wielded wrong, the scalpel could cause the patient to bleed out. He'd have to keep a close eye on her.

His body took that command in an immediate, literal way.

His gaze raked over her, from the light-brown curls that were draped over one shoulder, to the breasts that were proudly displayed in her clingy, satin dress. He continued down to the soft curves of her hips that led to the slit in her dress revealing a taut, muscular thigh leading to shapely calves. Christ if she wasn't the most beautiful journalist he'd ever seen—as evidenced by the bulge pressing against his slacks—but her pointed questions belied that she wasn't one who'd gotten by on her looks, either.

Then there was her flippant comment about her father being proud of her... What about her mother? And why, for the love of all he held holy, was she generating more questions than she asked?

Philip held his breath as Gregory answered a question about the royal family's history with photographs, or the lack of. He only exhaled when Gregory gave a satisfactory answer—not too much, nor too little so that it might invite any follow up. And it was the truth, mostly. His family had a longstanding tradition that predated the war with Russia, decreeing the royal family was not to be photographed or put into the news in any capacity other than official. Even then, they'd managed to skirt the lines of what could be deemed "official" quite effectively.

Sure, the Prince hadn't quite kept that end of his bargain after his breakup, since rumors of his frequent "relationships" intrigued readers and kept his name in the papers. But at least the family had kept photographs from circulating. It had been a Herculean task in the modern age of smartphones and tablets, though being a small sovereign country in a remote corner of the world hadn't hurt. He hoped they would be able to keep it up, at least for Gregory's sake.

Christ, this whole thing was a mess. When he found out who'd sent this viper gussied up in satin right to his home, he'd have their hide. Like he didn't have enough on his plate with everything else. Now he had to entertain this circus.

"Prince Gregory, I hope you don't find me uncouth for going this direction, but you know I can't just stick to the benign topics."

Benign? She'd been asking pretty intimate questions. Damning questions that if answered fully could sink everything he'd been working to build. And she considered them innocuous? His heart rate spiked, and a tremor he hadn't seen in a year shook his hands like they were leaves in autumn. He took three deep breaths that didn't do squat to calm the trembling that had now spread to his chest.

"Of course not," Gregory replied, putting his hand on Aurelia's.

Philip watched Gregory's thumb rub circles on the soft bit of flesh between Aurelia's fingers, heard her giggle in response to something else he said, too low for Philip to hear. The tremor turned to rage, hot and roiling inside his chest.

He didn't like watching Gregory's hand on the reporter's one bit. Regardless of how he felt about her being there in the first place, he couldn't deny the surge of electricity that had flung back and forth between them as if they were part of the same shorted circuit.

He wanted her, plain and simple.

He'd listen to the tough questions, to answers that might curse them all, but Gregory had better keep his hands off this woman. Besides, what if her playful flirting tricked Gregory into sharing something too intimate, too damning for her to print? He rubbed his temples, pressing against a headache that was building behind his eyes. Good Lord, why couldn't the editor have sent a balding, old man to cover the Prince?

Gregory's foot tapped against the table, then rested against Aurelia's exposed calf. *Oh, heck no.*

Philip took a step off the wall but was met with a hand across his chest. He turned, ready to unleash holy Hell on whomever had the audacity to lay a hand on him. This wasn't okay, none of it. If he could just go back to how things were a year ago, to who he was back then, he could fix everything.

"I just need to…" he started, but his gaze was met with the owner of the offending arm—his father's best friend, Petre, the head of the guard. The only man he'd ever let get away with laying a hand on him.

The eyes that stared back at him were not unlike what

Philip could recall of his father's. The same steel, the same hard set that watched unwavering and never flinched. The same cold gray that told a story.

"No, son. Let him be. This is his role to play and you've no business interfering with it." The voice matched the eyes—cold and heavy as steel.

"But do you see the way he's... he's—" Philip, meanwhile, sounded petulant, childlike.

"That's none of our concern. They're both adults, and well, she seems rather sweet. It wouldn't hurt Gregory to be with someone kind and smart for a change. Besides, you didn't like the direction the questioning was going, did you? Distracting our guest might be best for all of us, wouldn't you agree?"

That was the problem, wasn't it? Philip didn't want anyone to distract their guest. Anyone but him. Admitting that to himself added a level of confusion he didn't have the energy to wade through at the moment, especially because yes, he was worried about the distraction she'd cause. What if she distracted Gregory and he told her the precise reason he was there with her? Then, it didn't matter how much his body craved Aurelia. They'd all be toast. Petre was right, dammit. He needed to put his feelings for her—good and otherwise—out of his mind.

Sure, he wanted to spend time with Aurelia, figure her out, but at the same time, she infuriated him to no end. She'd been petulant and stubborn when he'd first introduced himself to her, and she was unwavering in her line of questioning instead of taking the less-than-subtle hints Gregory threw back at her.

In fact, she reminded him of the palace puppy he'd taken in as a child before his parents had found out—a sheepdog that didn't know the meaning of the word *quit*. He'd been just as annoyed with that cursed dog as he was with the journalist now. But when his parents had threatened to adopt the puppy out to a family that was around more, that had land for the pup to run, Philip had been so overcome with jealousy, imagining the puppy licking some other little boy's face, that he'd run away in the middle of the night, only to be brought home by Petre. He hadn't forgotten the lashes he'd received for his disobedience, which was another reason he backed down now and resumed his place against the wall.

Philip sighed. No, he couldn't get involved. As much as he wanted to ask—nay, *demand*—Gregory to back off, to leave Aurelia alone, he simply couldn't. The pang in his chest magnified tenfold when Aurelia doubled over laughing, Gregory's hand perched on her shoulder.

Jesus.

He didn't need this.

Not now, not when the King was out on his Amnesty tour and the Prince would be temporarily taking over his stateside duties in Aldonia. Not when Philip was just starting to feel the pull of his old position calling him out of his temporary retirement.

"Okay, so despite the fact your knowledge of American pop culture is scarily on point, I actually need to ask you something real. Would that be okay?"

"Of course, darling. Anything for you."

Philip's skin crawled with the sentiment from Gregory. None of Gregory's other conquests bothered him, so why this woman? Why now? He knew the answer, of course, but that didn't mean he had to like it.

"Okay. I need to address the rumors about the Queen."

"That's not a question, but I can confirm her pregnancy. A little girl, due soon."

"Yes, I'm actually aware of that, and congratulations to her and the King. But I want to know what happened between you and Queen Marjorie. Did she leave you for your brother? And if she did, can you talk me through what happened?"

Philip choked on a sharp intake of air, drawing everyone's eyes to him.

Crap.

He hadn't been expecting that. Aurelia's tone shifted; she was back to all business. Despite the fact her question shocked the heck out of him, and from the looks of it, Gregory as well, at least her interaction with Gregory was less intimate. He'd rather take the hits on the Queen's personal life than see Aurelia flirting with his best friend.

Not that he'd admit that to anyone else.

"Um, well, that's a story, isn't it? A long one, too. Gosh, do we have time, Philip?"

Gregory had used the code they'd come up with when an interview headed south, a signal that told Philip he'd better swoop in and rescue the poor man before he said something he shouldn't.

Philip cleared his throat.

"Ms. Beck? That's actually all the time we have this evening. The Prince has an engagement he cannot miss."

"That's a line of crap," she accused, her chest pushed forward, along with her chin. It took every ounce of Philip's resolve to not let his gaze wander down her body, especially since the pale-blue satin dress she wore left little to the imagination. Her curvy figure—all soft edges he wanted to run his hands down, to find the even softer folds he knew he'd discover if he was given carte blanche to explore—was in complete juxtaposition to her rough-around-the-edges personality. It was maddening. "You're helping him avoid having to answer the question, *sir*," she spat.

Somehow, every time the word *sir* came out of her mouth, it slapped him across the face like a curse. He was beginning to regret having her address him as such, which he would have bet all the money in his private account was her point. Wily vixen.

"Perhaps. But either way, the Prince is done for tonight. Ser Petre, can you see the Prince to his chambers?" Philip didn't miss the frown on Gregory's face as he got up to leave. He was actually sad to be leaving Aurelia.

Huh.

Philip shook his head. Another complication to be dealt with another time.

"I thought this was his room?" Aurelia asked as the door shut behind Gregory and Petre, who shot Philip a knowing glance on his way out. Relief flooded Philip's chest as her attention shifted from the interview. It was only temporary, though. She seemed incapable of leaving well enough alone.

"No, in fact, this is your room for the week."

Philip stifled an amused smile when her jaw dropped. Her cheeks turned a vivid pink, the color creeping down her neck and flushing her chest. His fingers itched to touch her skin, desperate to know if it would be cool to his touch, if it was as soft as it appeared. Her physical reaction to everything—the way she seemed to wear each emotion—made him react in kind. His slacks tightened around the zipper.

Jesus, what was wrong with him? She was just a woman, for Christ's sake. Even worse, an American, working-class woman there on business.

"But this, this…" she stumbled over the words, her hands waving in the air behind her, "This is too much."

"These are our guest quarters. If you're unhappy with the space, we can try to find something more suitable to your tastes." He tried not to feel guilty for enjoying the look of sheer discomfort on her face, but after how she'd behaved like a stubborn know-it-all earlier, he allowed himself the small pleasure.

"No. No, I mean, this is lovely. Thank you. But, um, my bags?"

"Will be brought up immediately. We've taken the liberty of making sure your preferred shampoos and creams were added to your powder room, but if you should need anything else, Ser Jaime will be on hand to assist you. Your itinerary is on the table by your bed. Get some rest—your day begins early, Ms. Beck."

"Thank you. But Philip? Sir?" Her tone was softer than when she'd spoken to him earlier, yet different still from the laid-back way she conversed with Gregory like they were old friends. This was the first time uncertainty crept into her voice, and it was all he could do to not close the small gap between them and take her in his arms. Where the compulsion came from, he had no idea, but it didn't sit well with him. He hadn't had a desire like that since he'd been left by his ex, and he'd sworn then he'd never let anyone else in like that again. *Ever.*

"What?" he snapped. He didn't mean for the word to come out as an admonition, but Christ if she didn't draw out the worst in him, magnify each of his weaknesses.

"How do you know what shampoo I use?"

He let a smirk tip the corners of his lips upward as he closed the distance between them. He inhaled the scent of lavender and mint and tried like heck not to notice her full, pursed bottom lip that she nibbled on.

"You aren't the only one who does their research, Ms. Beck."

"Touché," she said, her perfect, plump lips drawn up in a sneer. Never had that one snarky word seemed so sensuous. Or dangerous.

As Philip turned toward the door, he halted mid-step as if he'd run smack into an invisible wall. Without pausing to consider the ramifications of the word that followed, he whipped around and told Aurelia simply, "Stay."

She stared at him with the same expression his subconscious shot at her—a look of mild confusion mixed with curiosity.

"What's that supposed to mean? Where would I be going?"

When she rested her hands on her hips, drawing his gaze to the soft curves just barely covered by fabric, he groaned. The last shred of his resolve diminished, leaving him with half a hard-on and a bemused expression on his face. He closed the distance between them in a stride until he was a breath away from those lips that had him in a trance. Damn if they weren't the one thing keeping him there, grounded in place, wondering what they might do, or say next.

"Stay here," he added, not sure where he was headed with this asinine conversation until his brain picked up where other parts of him had clearly been leading the way before. "Stay here for the month. I'll give you the story you're looking for, answer the questions Prince Gregory wouldn't."

Crap. Where had that come from?

Her eyes hardened, creases marking her age where the rest of her looked to be no more than twenty. The maturity suited her personality, somehow made her more appealing. Suspicion lined her forehead, though, etched in her downturned mouth. He couldn't fault her for being more than a little concerned by his surprise proposal. It had shocked the heck out of him to hear the words coming out of his mouth just moments before.

"And why wouldn't he just offer up that information without you getting involved?"

That was the crux of it, wasn't it? Why would the Prince need the advisor to handle a simple PR story? It was at once a simple and complex question with a convoluted answer, one he'd have to share with her soon. But not tonight. Tonight, he had other desires that didn't include talking.

"Let's just say he and I have an arrangement."

"An arrangement? How mafioso of you." She flipped her curls over her shoulder and shifted her weight to one leg, jutting out a hip. Her eyes remained curious, but waves of distrust wafted off her slender but strong shoulders. "What's the catch?"

"The catch?" he asked, a corner of his mouth turned up in amusement. This might actually be fun if she accepted. Sure, she was obnoxious, a little know-it-all-ish, but she had a spark that could ignite some fire in a place that had been chilly for far too long. "Now who's acting like a gangster? I have no agenda, I promise." The sudden pressure of his erection against his slacks called out his lie as soon as it was out of his mouth.

Fine. So, he wanted her. Judging by the way her nipples cut through the bodice of her dress, he didn't seem alone in that desire.

"I don't believe you'd willingly give up all your state secrets just like that. What changed your mind from ten minutes ago when you whisked the Prince out of the room with some fake out-of-time story?"

What *had* changed? Not seconds before, she'd frustrated him to the point of anger, and now all he could think about was getting her in bed. It wasn't an unfamiliar feeling, the pull and push of a dangerous woman, and the risk of what he was about to do thumped against his chest like an irate rhino trying to escape. Last time he'd attempted something similar—a lifetime ago as far as he was concerned—it had blown up in his face and landed him alone and in a job he was as ill-suited for as he was perfect for the one he'd been forced to abdicate. Hardly an ideal situation to find himself in yet again.

Still...

This didn't have to be a repeat of *her*. He was fully capable of having a one-night stand and not making more out of it than that.

But that didn't answer her question, or the one his overactive subconscious screamed at him from the recesses of his brain. Why had he asked her to stay? Why had he promised her the story, with full intent to give it to her? Two dozen reporters in as many months had tried and failed at extricating the same information he was about to enthusiastically share with a woman he'd known for all of two hours.

By all accounts, it was a mistake, asking her to remain for a month. One that could have devastating ramifications for both him and Aldonia. So why didn't it feel that way?

Why did his heart thwart the fear and risk with a louder beat that only increased in strength when his gaze took in the stunning woman in front of him?

"I'm not sure, if I'm being honest." He chuckled, running his hands through his hair, and noted the lines around her eyes softened. Her lips curved into a smile, and Christ, if he had any doubts about her, or what he'd asked of her, they vanished on the light breeze that swept in from the balcony.

The air was heavy with the smell of new life in the desert—creosote and a hint of rain on the horizon. It was the smell of his childhood, the signal that used to alert him that spring term was almost over, that freedom loomed just on the periphery of his schoolbooks and tutors' terse lessons to pay attention. It had been far too long since he'd let the pulse of the land, *his land*, guide him, as it was there, in the guest suite with Aurelia.

Damn, it felt good.

Freedom and hope coursed through his veins as he placed a hand on Aurelia's shoulder. She was startled but didn't move to release herself from his touch. Instead, as he'd expected, heat built between their skin until he let his hand fall to his side, afraid if he waited longer, he'd singe them both.

"Well, I'd take a dose of honesty any day over the crap you pulled earlier." She laughed as well, and the mood shifted, lightened as if the heat from the desert beyond the walls of the castle burned through a heavy fog.

"I'm sorry about that. It's just that we pride ourselves on our discretion."

"Well, that's going to go out the window if you let me write my story, isn't it?"

"It will, but maybe it's time it did." He gazed down into her eyes that seemed composed of light and smoke rather than simple cells and proteins. They captivated him. *She* captivated him.

"What about photos?"

Philip bit back a grin, attempting—and failing—at serious. Jesus, he'd put himself right in the viper's pit, hadn't he? This woman was all work, no play. All the more reason to pull a page from Gregory's book and try to get her to join in the latter with him.

"Fine," he agreed, crossing his arms over his chest. When her breath hitched, her breasts grazed against the cotton of his shirt. Lust swirled in his chest, flooded south where it became painfully obvious how he felt about the pesky journalist. "But I get final approval on all images."

"Not the story, though?" She crossed her arms over her chest, mirroring his in a stand-off. All it did was close the millimeters between his body and hers. Another light breeze would be enough to press them together. This close, Aurelia's scent wrapped around him like a noose, cutting off his air. Lavender and spun sugar tickled his nose, entering his nervous system like an aromatic poison, shutting down his ability to think straight.

"No, that will be at your discretion. I'll give you the information and trust you tell it honestly, but you have to agree to stay the month—the *whole* month."

She seemed to consider this, worrying on her bottom lip again with her teeth. God, how he wanted to be those teeth, to take that bottom lip into his mouth and taste the lavender for himself.

"Fine," she countered. "But I want an exclusive with the Prince. Can you use your little *agreement* to make that happen?"

Philip swallowed back a retort that would have blown his whole proposal to hell.

"I'll make that happen. Now, let's talk salary."

"I already negotiated that with the Prince's head of staff, a woman named Patricia."

"Yes, but correct me if I am wrong. That negotiation only included the week's stay." It wasn't a question since he knew the inner workings of that deal by memory, so he wasn't going to pose it as such.

"That's partially correct. The stay was negotiated for a week, but the pay was for the story. It's more than sufficient."

"I don't agree. I'd be taking you away from other stories you could be writing. Opportunity cost, right? So, tell me—how much do you charge per story?"

Why did her cheeks color at the mention of money? If he didn't know better, he'd think he embarrassed her.

"I, um, contract at two thousand."

"Okay, so let's see. That's two thousand per week for four additional weeks of work. Throw in the exposure you are missing by writing exclusively for your magazine this month, why don't we call it eighty?"

She stared up at him, her lips parted and flushed, her cheeks matching them in pallor. Her exhale was warm on his chest, and the heat spread through his veins like whiskey, making him as lightheaded as well.

"Eighty what?"

"Eighty thousand."

She barked out a laugh completely devoid of humor and took a step backward, fury turning her gaze into a raging storm. More than her sudden change of mood, the loss of her presence irritated him. He wanted her close, as close as he could get her.

"That's ridiculous. What the hell are you playing at, *sir*?"

"I'll answer that if you answer a question of mine."

She glared at him, fire in her gaze, but she didn't respond.

"What happened to your mother?"

"Don't ever mention her again, do you hear me? She's off the table. Show me you understand, *sir*."

He nodded, his throat suddenly dry.

"Now tell me why you'd offer me a year's salary to do a cut-and-dry story or I'm out of here."

Her words were venom, searing his attempt at goodwill as they lashed against him. What had he done wrong?

Aside from the query about her mother, he'd only offered her fair market value for her work—what was so treacherous about that? At least he hadn't gone with his original offer of a hundred grand to try to lure her in. She'd probably have taken him to task for that. Jesus.

"Listen, you can think you're worth a smaller paycheck, but I won't keep the offer on the table for a penny less. You're a journalist, and if my instincts are right, you're a good one at that. If you do your due diligence with this story and go beyond the puff piece you were going to get out of Gregory, the story will pay for itself with PR for Aldonia. We're trying to secure a trade deal with the Republic of Georgia, and this press could be the thing that seals the deal. You'd be helping me, too."

"Who's to say I'll write anything remotely redeeming about the Prince or the country? So far, both have only moderately captured my interest." She was panting with anger, heat blossoming over every exposed inch of her flesh. Oh, that he could be the calm to cool her down. Instead, he only ever seemed to piss the woman off.

He sighed. "I only ask that you tell the truth. Whatever you learn, whatever that means to you."

Philip waited, fear rising like bile in his throat that she might say no. He'd put all his cards on the table, and she might fold before the game could even start. He'd already invested more than he intended, but little did she know how much he had to still give.

The hurricane raging across her features dissipated to a tropical storm, then the clouds parted, and the breath Philip was holding in came out in a rush. Tentatively, he took a step closer to her and counted it as a win that she didn't move away. Electricity buzzed between them again, firing off each nerve ending in Philip's arms and torso.

"Does that mean you'll take the deal?"

"I don't know why you're doing this, but I'm intrigued enough to accept your offer. Can we start tonight?"

He laughed, an unexpected and welcome sound that

filled the open room and cascaded out over the castle walls. When was the last time he'd let loose and laughed like that? It'd been too long, that was for sure. Leave it to this woman who drove him mad with frustration and wild with lust in equal measure to bring it out of him now, after all this time.

"Not tonight. I won't put you off, though, I promise. We'll start first thing tomorrow, but for tonight, celebrate with me."

He reached down and grabbed the half-finished bottle of wine on the table, then filled both glasses. There wasn't a chance he was leaving her side again to get a fresh glass for himself, so he handed off hers and took Gregory's for himself.

"What are we celebrating?" she asked, her voice thick and sensuous as the wine in her goblet. He'd take more of that any day over the expensive Georgian pinot noir they drank. He had a suspicion she'd send his head reeling more than any alcohol could.

"Our newly-forged partnership. May it be prosperous for us both." He ran a hand down her arm, watching in awe as a trail of goosepimples erupted underneath the path he drew along her satin skin. That he could have such an effect on her was heady, thrilling. He wanted more of it, more of her.

"Mmmmm," she hummed, clinking glasses with him. They sipped at the wine, neither breaking eye contact with the other. The air grew heavy with expectation. Aurelia's chest trembled, her chin quivered despite the warm air that circled around them, wrapping them in the desert heat.

Before he could make sense of what was happening, Aurelia had set her glass back on the table, and her hands were around Philip's neck, pulling him down to her.

"What the—" he began, but the sentence got lost as her mouth closed over his, the sensation and surprise of her full lips on his—*finally!*—rendering him speechless.

Her hands branded his cheeks with their heat, their

softness, and his fingers wrapped around the base of her head, tangling in her curls. They were as soft as the rest of her. Christ—she felt ethereal, made of air and scent and magic. How else could he explain the way she opened him up after being closed off for so long? He deepened the kiss, afraid that if he paused to breathe, the corporeal form awakening the dormant lust inside him would evaporate.

Any joy he felt as liquid, candied lavender swirled around his tongue was temporary, though. As abruptly as their kiss had begun, it was over, leaving him breathless and devastated. Aurelia pulled away from him, wrenching his heart in the process.

Her hair was wild, her gaze feral as it darted between him and the solid oak door to the suite as if she longed to run. Her chest rose and fell in short rapid bursts, her overall look reminding him of a trapped animal.

"I—" she began, the bottom of her eyelids brimming with moisture. He was frozen in place, fear paralyzing him. He'd messed up. But how? And how could he fix it? "I'm sorry," she said, her voice a whisper almost lost in the breeze.

"No," he said, taking a risk and pulling her close to him again. His pulse slowed as she rested her forehead on his chest. The world stopped spinning off its axis as her arms wrapped around him and squeezed. "You have nothing to apologize for," he spoke into her hair, inhaling her scent and committing it to memory.

"I didn't mean to do something so rash, so irresponsible, not especially after the incredibly generous offer you made me. I've never done anything like that before," she said, almost to herself.

"I'm glad you did."

She looked up at him, some of the moisture spilling over and dampening her cheeks. He hooked a finger under her chin and dipped down, brushing his lips over hers until they parted for him. As her mouth opened, his tongue found hers, tangling with it, and she moaned against him.

He teased her tongue out, ran his along her bottom lip, and finally knew the exquisite pleasure of taking it inside his mouth and gently raking his teeth over it. He growled, and both his hands wound in her curls as he kissed her with a passion he'd never felt before. Their kiss became separate from them, blossomed into something beyond them both.

A frenzy of escalation happened so quickly that Philip didn't know who moved first. All he knew was his fingers fiddled unsuccessfully with the zipper at the back of Aurelia's dress. It seemed stuck, stalling his desire to lay her bare.

Her palms had migrated under his dress shirt and pressed against his chest, her thumbs brushing against his skin with a delicacy that only increased his urgency.

"Just pull the dress down," she breathed, and he didn't wait for another invitation. He tugged at the fabric, cringing when it tore along the seam. Oh, well, that he could afford to replace. What he couldn't do was wait another minute to run his hands down Aurelia's skin, to test his theory that the parts of her she'd kept hidden were as succulent and tender as the rest of her.

In an instant, Aurelia stood there in nothing more than a strapless, nude bra and matching underwear, a lace-wrapped gift he didn't deserve but itched to unwrap all the same. His breath came in shallow, greedy gulps, and desire ached like an injury in his stomach and lower, where he stood at attention for the beauty in front of him.

A grin spread from her mouth to her cheeks, turning them a pale pink. She reached behind her and unclasped her bra, springing free her breasts, leaving Philip with his jaw open in appreciation.

Her skin was cream, with *cafe au lait* curls cascading over a smooth, flawless shoulder. It threw into sharp contrast the small, dark features embedded like jewels on her face. Deep, amber-colored eyes speckled with darker, chocolate flecks were set above ruby red lips that shined as if they were really polished stone. Aurelia was a Greek goddess, tantalizingly alive and beguiling—an Aphrodite there to lure him into oblivion.

He didn't think he'd mind one bit.

He kissed each eyelid, the tip of her nose, then her lips. As tempting as her sugar-coated mouth was, he continued south to her collarbone, trailed his tongue along the burnished surface, and didn't stop until he reached her breast, which he took into his mouth. He teased her nipple with his tongue until it hardened for him, then turned his attention to her other breast, giving it the same treatment until Aurelia moaned, her fingers tugging at his hair, pulling him into her.

He stood, and in a single move, he swung one arm under her knees, wrapped the other around her back, and scooped her into his arms. In a stride, he was at the four-poster bed where he sat her down as gently as he could. God knew he wanted to throw her down and ravage her perfect body until they both screamed with pleasure, but more than any other area of his life, he understood Aurelia required restraint.

He wanted this to be perfect for her.

Tucking his thumbs in the thin straps of lace around Aurelia's hips, Philip slid them off, depositing them at their feet. He placed his hands on her ankles and spread them so he could kiss the inside of her knee, then he moved up the length of her thigh, using his tongue to mark his trail. Aurelia whimpered in delight, which urged him on. When he arrived at her center, he traced her folds with his tongue and sucked at her opening until the whimpers became soft cries of delight.

Driven to meet her every desire, as well as those she wasn't aware she had, he rocked back on his heels and stood, stripping for her. She nodded her approval as he climbed on top of her. Concern flooded his system, though, realizing he was missing an integral item they would need to go any further. She must have seen the apprehension etched in his frown, because she wrapped her hands around his biceps and pulled him until the tip of his erection teased her opening.

"I'm covered. With, well, you know," she said, her cheeks blazing with heat.

He laughed, and a nervous giggle escaped from Aurelia. God, she was adorable. And forward thinking. He was having trouble recalling why he'd ever found her annoying as he ran his thickness up and down the apex of her thighs.

"Please," she begged, arching her back.

Philip growled and wasted less than half a second plummeting himself inside her warmth. His growl became a primal keen, and as he made love to Aurelia, he lost himself in her arms, her lips, her scent.

Hours later, having made her squeal with pleasure and come three times, he lay behind her, finally having caught his breath. His arm draped over the curve of her hip that he knew without a doubt he could draw from memory, and he traced lazy circles on her skin. Her breath was slowing down, matching his, when his gaze fell on the bedside table.

Her press pass for the dinner and cocktail party the night prior lay there along with a small change purse and lip gloss. He frowned, mulling over the past few hours. They'd been spent well, making love to a beautiful woman who'd captivated him from the moment she'd fallen into his arms at the party.

Still, that was the problem. She wasn't there for him. Or rather, she was, but not to do what they'd just finished doing. She didn't even know who he was.

Crap. He'd really screwed things up—not just for her, but for the story he hoped to tell her the next day.

As was quickly becoming habit with her, Philip bent down to Aurelia's ear and whispered in it before his conscience could stop him. At least he could fix one of those problems then and there.

"I am the Prince, Aurelia. The real Prince of Aldonia."

When she didn't move, but just sighed and replied, "The Prince. Mmmmm," guilt wrenched at his heart. He was normally so calculated, so intentional with every move he made in his personal life as well as when it came to doing what was best for the country. Yet, ever since she'd walked through the palace doors, he'd thrown caution to the wind and acted like Gregory, as if he was free from the consequences of his actions.

It wasn't fair to her, nor to the country, which had suffered because of his previous relationship as it was.

He needed to put the journalist out of his mind, save letting her do the job she'd come there to do. It might undo him not to run his hands through her hair, trail his fingers along her jawline, but it had to be done. He was second in line to run his country, dammit. It was high time he started acting like it.

"I need to go. It wouldn't do well for the staff to find me here come morning."

She giggled, her eyes still closed. "Yes, the Prince in my bed, he-he." She was seconds from succumbing to sleep. He could see it in the easy way her breath filled and emptied her perfect chest. Slipping from the sheets he'd once thought couldn't be matched in their comfort magnified the ache he'd had before he touched her skin, rendering all other surfaces rough in comparison. How was he supposed to leave her there, alone? It hurt to even imagine it. Christ, this didn't bode well for the month that would follow.

He kissed her shoulder and slipped on his clothes in painful silence before dipping low and pressing his lips to hers once more.

"Goodnight. Sleep well, my dear, and have the sweetest dreams." He paused before adding, "Forgive me for what I must do tomorrow."

She murmured something in reply that was lost to the hum of the fan overhead and the pulse that raced in his ears.

With that, Philip strode from the room, careful to keep his clipped stride until he shut the door on Aurelia, on the only time he'd felt himself, felt good in years.

When he was certain the door was shut tightly behind him, the sentry stoic in his guard of her room, Philip leaned back against the stone wall and exhaled the remainder of a breath he didn't know he was holding in. Goosepimples covered his arms and chest despite the heat of the early morning. He held his hands in front of him at hip's height. The tremor had returned, and he knew from experience it wouldn't dissipate as quickly this time around.

Though he'd whispered to Aurelia to sleep well, to have good dreams, that wasn't in the cards for him. No, his world had been upended by her sudden presence in his life. As his imagination went rogue, imagining her naked, supple body wrapped in his sheets behind the thick slab of wood that separated them, he was certain.

Rest was the last thing in store for him that night.

KRISTINE LYNN

CHAPTER THREE: ROYAL TREATMENT

Aurelia slept as well as she had since she was a child, wrapped in safety and comfort beyond her wildest imagination. The satin-covered pillows and blankets, the cool breeze that covered her from the patio, the hum of the overhead fan—all of it combined with her exhaustion from travel and made sleep not only inevitable, but delightful.

Well, that and the ridiculously incredible lovemaking hadn't hurt.

Oh, God. That had really happened, hadn't it?

She pressed the heels of her palms against her eyes, hoping it would force the memory out of her thoughts.

Instead, images as bright as the desert sun and powerful enough to burn her retinas with the pictures flooded the back of her eyelids, and heat settled low in her abdomen. She pulled the covers over her head and screamed.

She'd kissed Philip. Kissed him, and then let that one, horribly irresponsible decision evolve into wrestling naked with him on her first night in the castle. If there was a Hell for journalists, she'd just secured her place there for eternity.

Because there was no way taking an assignment and then sleeping with a member of the staff was the right thing to do.

It hadn't felt wrong, though—that was the most concerning aspect of the whole night as far as she was concerned. She'd acted on impulse, something she hadn't done in years, maybe more. But while she'd expected to feel immediate remorse, instead, she'd been shocked to discover how right, how indefectible Philip had felt in her arms.

Still…

It couldn't happen again. Not if she wanted to leave the castle with a story in a week—no, a *month!* She'd conveniently forgotten how their conversation had started once the Prince left the room the night before. Philip had offered her an exclusive story—photos included—if she agreed to stay the month.

An entire month. With a man she couldn't keep her greedy hands off for two hours. She'd need to gain some self-control, and fast, if she wanted to be able to put his body out of her mind long enough to do her freaking job.

She could do that, surely. She was a professional, after all. What had been a complete and utter lapse in judgment would surely look better in the pale light that filtered through the satin drapes that separated her from the rest of Aldonia.

Plus, her initial impression of him—statuesque physique notwithstanding—wasn't too far off. He was controlling, manipulative, and obnoxiously stoic. If she could just call those images up at will instead of his hands on her breasts and hips, his smile shining down on her like the sun, his tousled hair after making love, his stupidly tanned and washboard stomach that looked computer generated it was so perfect…

She shook her head violently, trying again—and

desperately failing a second time—to eradicate the night before from the cache of recollections in her subconscious. The thing was, Philip wasn't the controlling, manipulative jerk she'd met at the party when they'd been alone together in her suite. He'd been as attentive and giving a lover as she'd ever had.

Ugh.

That wasn't why she was there, though. She was a journalist with a deadline and if she didn't get this story, then, well... The consequences of that were too dire for her to think about. At least that sobered her right up and tucked Philip's abs deep into the recesses of her mind where they belonged.

A wave of resolve flushed out the remnants of lust from the night before as Aurelia slid her feet out of bed and set them on the cool stone floor. Her toes curled in delight at the dramatic shift in temperature compared to the air. It was time to check out this country she'd only seen photos of on the internet. While she was at it, she sent off a quick text to her dad to let him know she was safe and well. She wouldn't allude to how well she was doing, though. That she'd save for a dish session with Lily at some point.

Okay. What to do today... *Don't think of Philip. Get dressed. Get your notes. Do your job.*

Since the second item on her list was decidedly easier than the first, she went to grab a clean outfit from her suitcase only to find it had been emptied and stowed away in the back of a closet that was bigger than her whole apartment.

All her clothes had been hung on satin hangers or folded and placed on silk-lined shelves. When had someone moved her things, and most importantly, why? She was more than capable of hanging her own clothes.

She hadn't brought as many outfits as were hung up, though. And nothing as nice as... She fingered a cotton blouse that may as well have been made of air it was so light. This wasn't hers. Neither were the slacks hung above it, nor the gowns beside them. And the shoes, encrusted in jewels and tall enough to send her careening to her death if she dared try them on? Yeah, not hers by a long shot.

So, whose were they, and why were they dispersed amongst her meager and threadbare belongings?

Groaning at the injustice of the juxtaposition between her lifestyle and whomever owned the ritzy apparel in the closet, she slipped on a white tank top and matching linen pants, pairing them with a turquoise necklace and matching earrings from the trip out west with her parents. She hadn't wanted to go on that road trip because if her father got the job, it would mean leaving her friends behind. However, she'd been blown away by the beauty of the red rocks and canyons as wide as they were deep. Her mother had purchased the jewelry for her as a souvenir, and since then, Aurelia had brought them on every trip as a reminder that some of the best things in life came from change, even the unexpected kind.

After tying her hair in a simple knot and adding a brush of mascara to her tired eyes, she felt better, more in control than when she'd awoken and been assaulted with flashbacks of her tryst with the advisor.

As she stepped out from the thin veil onto the patio, the last of the images of Philip evaporated into the sublime expanse before her. The countryside stretched in every direction as far as she could see and was so totally unlike what she'd imagined that her breath caught in her throat. Regret pushed against her chest as she wished—for the hundredth time in as many days—her mother could be there with her to see the majesty of this place.

Desert flowers in colors brighter than anything that bloomed on the east coast blanketed the undulating hills and valleys, and were punctuated by a long, serpentine swathe of trees. Were they cottonwoods? There must be a river hidden beneath their canopy, which would explain the smell of water that permeated the air. There was no doubt the castle sat squarely in the middle of an endless desert, but just as she'd been in Arizona, she was surprised by how much life it boasted.

As if on cue, a small family of feral pigs trotted out of the scrub brush closest to the palace walls, the smallest squealing as he was left behind by his older siblings and parents. Aurelia giggled and called out, "Hurry up, little one." She tugged her phone out from the small bag she'd packed with water, snacks, pen and paper, and a couple of the errant ChapSticks from the night before and snapped a photo of the little family before they disappeared over a ridge.

"Remember, I have final approval of all photos," came a voice that shot straight to Aurelia's core, liquifying it and the strength she'd built up to try and resist it.

She spun around only to face something brighter than the sun reflecting off the desert floor, and hopefully just as likely to be a mirage. Philip stood at the entrance to the vast patio, donning linen pants not dissimilar to hers and a tan button-down cotton shirt with the sleeves rolled up over his bronzed, sinewy forearms. She swallowed back a lump of desire that built in her throat.

He looked more decadent, more regal in the relaxed clothing than he had in his dapper suit the night before. It was both alarming and dizzying, seeing him there just hours after they'd made love, and looking like sin incarnate to boot.

Curse him for making this harder than it had to be, for making her feel more out of place than she already did.

She flinched when his hand rested on her shoulder. God help her, but no matter how hard she tried, Brian's influence on her persisted, even across an ocean.

"I'm sorry. Did I hurt you?"

"No," she said, trying on a smile. "It's just a…reaction I have. Sorry."

His scrutiny was unnerving, but even more so was the scent he carried with him, sweet and heady.

"Don't ever apologize for what you didn't do."

She nodded.

"What was his name so I can add him to the list of public enemies of the state? Any man who hits a woman deserves it brought back upon himself tenfold."

"Brian. How did you know?"

His gaze wandered over the desert in front of them. "The Queen. The former King, rest his soul, wasn't always the kindest man. But he learned. I'm terribly sorry anyone ever hurt you."

"Don't apologize for something you didn't do," she quipped, shooting him a grin she hoped would add some levity to their morning. And were they ever going to talk about the night before?

"Touché. Anyway, no photos." He winked back at her and yeah, they should probably talk sooner rather than later so she didn't jump him again. He was making it harder and harder not to.

"I wouldn't break that rule," she stated matter-of-factly, the rule she had broken by sleeping with him hanging in the air.

He smiled, and the flash of white juxtaposed against his tan skin sent fire roiling in Aurelia's stomach.

"Good morning, by the way," he told her, his voice tentative but kind. His stance reflected a careful approach, as if waiting to see how she behaved before he reacted.

"It is," she said, meaning it. How could it not be when it began in a place as beautiful as Aldonia? "I had no idea your country was so stunning. I feel bad for underestimating its beauty."

His gaze cut through her, scarring her with its intensity. Power wafted off him in shimmering waves as if he were made of the land below them. Why didn't she get the same impression when she was around Prince Gregory?

"We're all guilty of overlooking beauty. The important thing is to appreciate it when we realize its existence." His eyes didn't leave hers as he spoke. He took his time appraising her as if she were a piece of art he considered adding to the palace collection, starting at her thatched sandals and making his way up to her glossed lips, where his gaze lingered. He licked his own lips, causing her skin to flush with heat.

Desire kicked against her ribcage, desperate to be let out.

"Yes, um. Well, I appreciate it, that's for sure. I'd like to see more of it, but I think we should get started on the story. Did you get a chance to talk to the Prince about my extended stay?"

If she could just keep her eye on the prize, it would make it easier to let thoughts of unbuttoning Philip's cotton shirt and running her hand over the coarse dark hair peppered over muscled, sculpted flesh fall to the back of her mind.

Well, maybe.

Philip's brow furrowed, and panic bubbled up in Aurelia's chest. Was he going to tell her the deal was off? That because she'd acted like a harpy and slept with the advisor on her first night at the castle, she couldn't be trusted?

"It's fine if I can't stay. I know I messed up last night. If the Prince wants me gone—"

Philip was by her side in two strides. He wrapped one arm around her waist and pressed a finger to her mouth before dipping his head and using his lips to silence her instead.

"Shhhh," he whispered against her mouth. He tasted of coffee and chocolate, and her stomach growled with hunger for more than just a deepening of the kiss.

When was the last time she'd eaten?

Philip laughed at the sound and pulled back from her. Before mortification could set in at her body announcing its needs at full volume, he strode over to the phone and picked it up, barking a demand that included coffee and a list of foods that made Aurelia's mouth water be brought to her suite.

Mixing with the acid in her empty stomach, confusion set in, making her nauseated. Philip must have seen the way the color drained from her face because he brought her to a chaise lounge on the patio and set her on it as delicately as he'd placed her atop the feather mattress the night before.

Why was Philip demanding anything of anyone? Why wasn't the Prince there, checking in with her? As they had the night before, questions stacked up between her and the advisor, making it hard to see him clearly. She needed to focus, but her eyes watered in the sun.

"You need to drink more water than you're used to out here. The heat is deceptive, as is the power of the sun." He rubbed her shoulders, cooling them with his skin, but branding her, nonetheless.

"You just ordered breakfast," she stated, confused.

He nodded, his brow still drawn, his lips pressed in a tight line.

"Yes. You're clearly hungry, so I figured we should eat here before we get to work."

"But you ordered it, I mean ordered someone. And they listened to you."

He nodded again, but the creases lining his forehead smoothed, and his lips curved into a tight smile.

"How much do you recall from last night, Aurelia?"

Her head spun—whether from the heat or the inquiry, she couldn't be sure. Either way, she was distracted, lightheaded.

"Aside from the obvious?" she quipped.

Philip nodded.

"Yes. Aside from that. Before I left, I told you something, something important. Do you remember what I said?" His voice had taken on a caring, paternal quality, but there was something dangerous behind it, an edge that belied nerves he'd not shown to her before. That sent a tremor coursing through her body that only worsened as her dream from last night came back to her with a crashing clarity.

She'd been lying in a field of clover, a bubbling brook behind her that she could only see, not hear, and two horses were tied up nearby. It was nearing sunset because the light was soft, the colors in the sky sharp. Philip had been lying next to her, his hands trailing up and down her arm until a faceless sentry had sprinted into the clearing. Even though she couldn't read his expression, it had been one of alarm she'd felt emanating from his rigid stance.

He had buzzed and beeped, a robotic language she couldn't speak, but somehow understood.

We need you, Your Highness. There's an emergency up at the palace.

She hadn't been surprised in the dream that Philip had leapt to his feet to answer the call because he'd been, of course, the Prince the sentry was speaking to.

He is the Prince. She'd known it then as deeply as she knew it now. The tremor turned her insides to jelly, her skin to ice despite the near-hundred-degree air that stifled her ability to breathe, to think.

"You remember, don't you?"

She nodded, even as she realized it changed everything, made her world as she knew it obsolete.

"You're the Prince," she whispered. Though the words had come out quiet, serene, inside her chest, it was as if she'd screamed them at full volume.

"I am," he replied, taking her hand in his and standing her up.

She stared at his chest, her mind murky and sluggish as she tried to process the implications of this, not just for her, but for her story, for his country.

"Why?" she asked as he walked them inside the bedroom. The air was cooler, but Aurelia still felt overheated, disoriented.

"Off the record?" he asked, a hint of a smile tugging at his lips.

How hadn't she seen it sooner? Of course, he was the Prince. Who else but him, with his impossibly high standards and impenetrable strength, could rule a country?

She glowered at him through thick lashes, frowning at his attempt at humor. "Not likely."

He chuckled. "Yes, well, I didn't think I'd get away with it, but no harm in trying, hmm?"

"Why?" she asked again.

Before he could answer, the door opened and an older woman carrying a tray of coffee came in, a man in close pursuit with an even bigger tray laden with fruits, pastries, and—oh yes!—*bacon.*

Her mouth watered as she stood to greet the welcome guests, whose glances shifted between her and Philip. Philip only smiled, thanked them, and helped them transfer the breakfast to the dining table where she'd interviewed Gregory—who was clearly the wrong person to talk to after all—the night before.

"She knows," Philip told them, winking at the woman.

Surprise, then elation flitted across the stout face of the woman, but the gentleman maintained his composure. What had Aurelia's face looked like as the truth had dawned on her features?

"Oh, dearie. I knew you were strong enough to let it go. Welcome back, sire."

Let it go? The warning bells flared again, a welcome intrusion against the cacophony of noise that had distracted her from her job since the night before.

"I'll talk to you more about it later, Patricia. Until then, thank you for the food. I'll come by the kitchens later."

She bowed her head and retreated the way she'd come in, gesturing for the other gentleman to follow her.

When the doors shut softly behind them, Aurelia turned to Philip, her mouth open and ready to pelt him with a list of questions that grew the longer she sat there, silent.

Why pretend he wasn't the Prince?

What was he "getting over" and why did he have to abdicate the throne—even temporarily—to do that?

Why was Gregory chosen to act as a royal in disguise?

Who else knew?

Most importantly, why did he let her kiss him without knowing who he was? This question bothered her most. She'd kissed a Prince, then let him ravish her body in ways that made her flush with heat to recall. Surely, this was a much larger transgression than just sleeping with a royal advisor. Could she be tried for treason for such a royal screwup?

Before she could let a single inquiry pass her lips, though, Philip shook his head, nodding to the food.

"Patricia will see me beheaded before you enjoy her food less than piping hot. Sit. Eat. Then I'll tell you everything."

Even if Aurelia could muster up an argument against that, her stomach roared that she'd better not dare. Scowling, she sat down and shoved a croissant into her mouth instead, choosing to ignore the smug grin that spread across Philip's face as she ate.

Any misgivings about having slept with Philip—*Prince* Philip—were gone when she discovered one of the many perks that came with it. The food the morning after. Aurelia didn't know if she'd ever tasted anything so simply divine as the royal spread before her. Grapes that were fit to burst with flavor were preceded by pastry that was made more of light and air than flour and butter. She swallowed them all down with a creamy coffee layered with a hint of butterscotch, her favorite.

Then a question popped into her head that had nothing to do with the Prince's bait and switch.

"Whose clothes are in the closet?" she asked, her mouth full. She couldn't have cared less about acting like a starving child who hadn't eaten in a month, crumbs falling from her lips. She was ravenous, and until she got answers to at least some of her questions, she refused to act on ceremony.

Confusion flashed across his chiseled features again.

"They're yours. I had Patricia hang them this morning while you slept."

"Yes, thank you. I saw that, but I meant the gowns and fancy tops, and the shoes—they look fit for the Queen."

"They're yours as well. If you're going to be here a month and attend royal functions, you need to fit in."

Aurelia's initial reaction was anger. She hadn't asked to attend any functions, nor go anywhere the clothes she'd arrived in wouldn't do. She shared as much with him.

"I'm sorry," he said, throwing his shoulders back in defiance as she popped a mouth-watering piece of bacon in her mouth. "I didn't mean to offend you, but you have to see the practicality of the wardrobe I provided you."

She did, and she saw that he meant well. She also saw that he'd never understand how insulting it was to be reduced to "not good enough" because she didn't wear clothes a king or queen would. Instead of arguing her point, which she knew would get her nowhere when it came to having her questions answered, she simply said, "Thank you."

"You're welcome." He frowned though, and Aurelia got the sense she'd been the one to offend him.

"What's the matter?" she asked.

"It's just not often that someone surprises me, and you continue to do so. I meant to ask you; did you like the gift I left on the washroom counter?" He looked down at her bare wrist and frowned. "Did it not match, or isn't it your taste either?"

Aurelia followed his gaze to her naked wrist, confused.

She didn't recall seeing a box. Rather than answer his question, she hopped up, grabbing another piece of bacon to go, and skipped to the bathroom. There, in the center of the marble countertop, was a small, plainly wrapped box.

Aurelia made her way back to the table and opened it.

She couldn't contain the smile that erupted at seeing the gold arc with minuscule geometric shapes cut from it. It was almost identical to the candle shade in her room, by far her favorite piece in the palace so far.

"It's beautiful." And it was. Like everything else in the palace, it reeked of understated elegance and was much more to her taste than the clothes and shoes. Philip beamed with pride as she held the bracelet up to the skylight, light catching it so shapes formed on the wall. "You all have a way with light."

"We have enough of it that sometimes it's blinding. One can begin to take it for granted, not unlike being around exquisite beauty for too long. We bend it, shape it, so we never forget the simple joys that surround us."

Aurelia didn't know what to say to that. It was stunning, but she already felt awkward having accepted most of an annual salary for a story she was going to write for a fraction of the price. And then the clothes? He'd better not be buttering her up to paint Aldonia—or him— in a more flattering light. She couldn't be bought.

Attempting an agreeable smile, she nodded.

"I love it. I'll treasure it, especially during a New York winter. I could use more light every February."

Philip chuckled and took the bangle from her with one hand, then held her wrist with the other.

His touch was like a bolt of electricity right to her heart and the pit of her abdomen at the same time. She peered up at him and remembered how mesmerized she was the night before as she gazed into the blue-green jewels that stared down at her now. They were less of a storm now, softer around the edges, which somehow added brightness to the already glowing irises. He slipped the bracelet over her hand but didn't release either.

"We've crafted them into a national emblem, and as you can see, if you wear it the opposite way, the arc faces out. The way you wear it tells the world whether your heart is taken or not."

"Which way am I wearing it now?" she asked, her voice a whisper as his face drew closer to hers. Her heart beat wildly in her chest, and she worried it would start echoing off the palace walls it screamed so loudly in his presence.

"Your heart is open to whatever comes. Should I leave it this way? Or are you spoken for?"

Hope lined his voice, but she couldn't make sense of which way he wanted her to answer. Ever the enigma, this man.

Aurelia shook her head, unable to break the trance Philip's close proximity had her in. "I'm open. My heart is open."

Why was she so quick to dismiss any idea of a fling at home, only to be more than willing to let Philip in her bed? She'd sworn off bad boys, but there didn't seem to be a force in the universe to keep her from lusting after this strange man in an even stranger country.

Her subconscious reminded her less-than-gently that she was there for work.

Nothing else.

Her mother's voice chimed in, though, with a gentle tone that used to send Aurelia straight to sleep when she was a child.

He's not a bad guy, hon. Give him a chance to show you who he is beneath the surface. You don't have much to lose.

She cleared her throat, shook her head, and pulled her hand free. As much as the small morsels of advice from her mother unnerved her, caused more pain than Aurelia thought she could endure, she also feared the day she stopped hearing them.

"Shall we start the interview then? I think I've got more than enough questions to last the month," she joked, hoping to lighten the mood.

He laughed.

"How about we walk and talk. I'd love to show you where you'll be living this month. If you liked the desert beyond our walls, just wait 'til I show you what we're hiding inside them."

She agreed and gathered her small bag and some sunglasses at the last minute as she glanced out the sheer drapes at the brightly lit landscape and then followed Philip to the edge of the room.

She reached out to open the large wooden door, but a member of the guard beat her to it.

"Thank you." She walked out, the guard nodding curtly in response. "Do they always do that?" she asked Philip.

"Only if they want to keep their job," he replied, a tight smile on his face.

"I'm perfectly capable of opening a door and I'm sure they have plenty more pressing matters to attend to, your safety for one," she spat, not caring about the haughty tone she took with him. She loved the space, the grandeur of the property she'd seen so far, but there was something so old-fashioned about having servants wait on her hand and foot. That wasn't something she could never get used to.

"Well, this is part of their job."

"I see that, but it seems superfluous in this day and age, doesn't it?"

"I hadn't considered it."

Of course, he hadn't. She let the dismissal roll off her shoulders, though, more determined than ever to enjoy the day and get answers to the myriad questions that were starting to overwhelm her.

Philip took Aurelia's hand and led her down a hallway she didn't recognize. His hand was rough, strong, not unlike her father's. He was a man who worked for a living, she could feel that in his calluses, his strength. So why had he been hiding out as an advisor? And for how long?

She hung on every word Philip spoke as he talked idly about his decision to hand over temporary care of the country to Gregory, who was in fact, the advisor who'd saved Philip's life a few years earlier. The real shock, however, came when Philip admitted that he and Gregory had been childhood best friends. Trying to picture Philip as a young man running amok on his property, getting into trouble with his closest friend, was more than Aurelia's imagination could drum up.

Gregory's father had managed the royal stables, and his sister—the student Gregory had mentioned at Columbia—had been in love with Robert, Philip's older brother and the future King. When they came of age, Gregory was given the title of guard at his own request, then advisor later on when, on duty, he'd usurped a plan to assassinate Philip and caught the man responsible. Philip still hadn't gotten to the why of the whole story—the reason he'd left the throne in the first place—but they had time, and this story was more than enough to sate her curiosity for now.

It was a tale of epic heroism, and at once, everything made sense. Why the two men seemed to speak a language all their own. Aurelia thought of Lily, and an ache at not seeing her friend for a month spread through her chest.

After what seemed like a mile of palace hallways and passages behind them, Philip led her out of the corridor into the sunlight. The view spread before her like a bounty, and Philip erased her homesickness with a simple wave of his hand.

The most majestic wall of emerald green she'd ever seen, sunlight glinting off each leaf, each bud, rose in front of them. The wall was alive with movement, teeming with color and light. With life. Small insects buzzed from plant to plant, nourishing themselves on the jewels gifted them by the flowers. Birds chirped as they swam in and out of the paths as if they were caught in a current.

The whole scene appeared to go on for days, unmolested by other buildings or structures, save a small gazebo off to the right.

"The Royal Gardens, Ms. Beck," Philip said, waving his arms over the expanse of land.

A floral aroma so intoxicating she felt drunk off one deep inhale assaulted her. It was her mother's garden, but on a commercially expansive level. Her heart struggled not to cry out with the pain of loss that came with the beauty.

There were colors she'd only seen in paintings—pinks, blues, reds that looked as fake as the mountains behind them did—though both were as real as the man whose hand was wrapped in hers, calming her flutter of emotions. It was a welcome change from his constant appraisal of her.

"I never tire of this view, but I have to say there's nothing as special as seeing it through new eyes. Do you like it?"

She turned to face him, her cheeks flushed with heat only partially due to the desert beyond the gardens. "This is incredible, Philip. I love them. My mother would love them."

"I thought she was off the table," he teased.

"She was, but this... she would love this so much. I don't mind sharing her with you if you've shared this much with me."

"What happened to her?"

Before she could respond, he tucked her hair behind her ear, the touch both gentle and familiar.

"She passed away a few years ago. My father is a good man, and I know he wants to be there for me however he can, but we both sort of lost our way when she died. Anyway, she was somewhat of an expert gardener and would have been in heaven to see what you've done here.

"I can't take the credit, but thank you. And thank you for sharing her with me. I'm sure she's proud of you."

"I hope so. So, um, tell me more about this space. If you didn't do the digging and troweling, who did?" She needed not to focus on her mother or she'd break down before she finished the tour. It was all she could do to keep it together as it was.

"The gardens have been in the family for nine generations. Before that, the land belonged to Russia and they were fields worked by slaves. All of those slaves were offered amnesty when the royal family took over rule, and to share their appreciation, they built these gardens. Many of their descendants still work for the castle today in the stables or kitchens. A few have made their way to the royal guard."

"What about you? Your family? You mentioned a brother, who I am assuming is the King?"

"He is." And just like that, the smile was wiped from Philip's face and a shadow fell across it.

"Do you have any other siblings?"

"None. Just Robert."

Aurelia playfully slugged Philip on the shoulder. "You know, if you want me to talk to you, you're going to have to be more than monosyllabic."

"Where's the fun in making it easy on you?" He winked, and a flame ignited in Aurelia's abdomen. It moved south, fire consuming each limb, each cell. His crystal blue-green eyes seemed to delve deep into her soul, assessing who she was beyond her job, her writing, her sass. Did he like what he saw? "Would you like to get out of here?"

Get out of there? Never. Not unless that somewhere answered the calling that awoke in her when she looked too deeply into his sea-green eyes. Her body, acting on muscle memory, buzzed with desire when she recalled what their bodies felt like pressed together. Her gaze traveled to Philip's strong chest, just inches away from her lips. Her lips went dry, the moisture sucked south, where it dampened her underwear.

Christ on a bicycle.

She mentally slapped her subconscious that apparently had a libido which, if left unchecked, would get Aurelia in trouble this month.

"Where would we go that would be better than these gardens? I could spend a year here and never want to leave."

"I'd like to take you somewhere we don't allow

journalists or tourists. These will be here the whole month."

The whole month. Time stretched before her, ripe with possibility now that she'd accepted Philip's proposal.

"Well, I'm both a journalist and first-time Aldonia visitor, so you'd better be absolutely sure before you take me. I'm as curious as a cat with only one life left."

"That's why I know you'll appreciate it."

Philip moved slowly enough to allow Aurelia to keep up without too much effort. While they walked, he told her about the castle's history, starting with the gardens. When he explained that his parents were killed in a small plane accident five years prior, that the gazebo was built by him and Robert in their honor, Aurelia caught the hitch in his breath. It was infinitesimal, but she'd seen it. He wasn't as stoic as he let on.

Philip didn't seem to notice her studying him as he continued on about the castle.

Similar to much of the countryside, it had to be rebuilt after the war. Bombs had destroyed all but a small part of the compound, including the main fortress. He explained why it was important to retain a stronghold in the south while the King reigned in the north at the capital. The locals needed to see a constant royal presence so they were reminded that they were looked after, that just because they were rural, it didn't mean that they weren't integral to the success of the country.

Aurelia nodded along, but stress creeped up her shoulders and furrowed her brow as he talked.

"It's a grand notion, but I saw the way the people live outside the castle walls on my way in last night. There's still extreme poverty, still work to be done."

"Sure, but it's the same in every country, isn't it? A disparity between the rich and poor?"

"That doesn't make it right. How can you all feel comfortable living like kings in here while children starve outside your walls?"

"We *are* kings. Should we not work with what we were given? And besides, we can't help the families that don't want to help themselves."

Philip's voice had gone gravelly, while Aurelia's was an octave higher than normal.

"What about those that can't help themselves? What do you do for them?"

"Enough. We do enough. Jesus, Aurelia, is anything we do enough to meet your standards?"

"My standards aren't anything compared to that of the country. They want clean water, education, food on their tables, to go to the doctor and not pay their annual salary for treatment. That's not asking much, is it? Or do you not care what happens to your people?"

"You're impossible."

"Maybe, but that doesn't mean I'm wrong. Where are we?" she spat when Philip stopped at a doorway that was, compared to the rest of the castle and grounds, unassuming; it consisted of plain wood with metal hinges. No adornments, no carvings. Because of this, it stood out like a lake in the middle of the desert.

"Open it. See for yourself."

Though it was meant as an offer, it came out as a command. So he was back to being infuriating. Oh, goody. At least her desire to press him up against a castle wall and have her way with him was long gone.

Aurelia shoved the door open and came face-to-face with more books than she'd seen in any public library combined. She inhaled deeply, a smile of appreciation breaking through her repeated agitation with Philip. Every time he seemed close to driving her off the edge of annoyance with his over-confident, demanding attitude, he brought her to a place as close to heaven as she could imagine. It was a good tactic. Especially this place. Laid out in front of her was a library unlike any other she'd visited.

Books upon rows of books.

Muted red and silver spines twinkling with the light they let in.

And, oh, God, the scent of paper, new and old.

It called to her, drawing her further inside the room. The ceilings rose higher than the outside of the structure let on, and more light poured in than had a right to. Much of it was shaped into the now-standard crescent moons and stars Aurelia had grown fond of.

It was a treasure, plain and simple.

She turned back toward him, her mouth agape.

"It's stunning. But don't think I'm going to drop our conversation just because you brought me to my favorite place on Earth. We're coming back to your policies later. But for now," she said, softening her approach, "can I explore? It's incredible."

"So are you," he whispered so softly she almost missed it. He stood close enough that his scent—all musk and man—made her dizzy. What did he mean by that?

"Um, why don't you invite anyone here?" she asked ignoring his comment. "It's a library. I guarantee you any journalist you've met has seen books before."

"Not these books."

"Why? What makes them so special?"

"See for yourself. You know, for a so-called journalist, you want a lot of information handed to you."

She shook her head, gave her best scowl, her cheeks and forearms red with heat. Times like this she wished she believed in violence. She could smack this man he was so infuriating, though that would probably send her to the gallows if such a place still existed. She moved closer, inhaling deeply, trying to imprint the musky scent in her memories. Her nose brushed the cracked leather of a spine and she gasped.

"Is this...?" she asked, her hand covering the surprise etched on her mouth.

Philip nodded.

"All first editions. Amazing, aren't they?"

"They're a dream. Who's been collecting them?" Shakespeare, Yeats, even modern novels like Kingsolver lined the infinite shelves. It was the most impressive collection she'd ever seen. The literary part of her yearned to take one out, to delicately thumb through the pages, but she couldn't imagine where to start.

"All of us, but they're my passion project, actually. Ever since I was little, I've loved to read and be read to, so my family started the collection, and for the past decade and a half, I've kept it up."

"Have you thought of donating these to the country's library? I read online Aldonia gives every citizen access to public libraries. It would be a step in the right direction for offering your world to them. Think of how good you will look when you resume your throne—how the country will thank you for it."

"Do you ever just stop and enjoy something without trying to fix or change it?" he asked. His voice was all frustration—in another life, she imagined he'd be a good vice principal of a middle school.

She shrugged, a smile on her face. She just couldn't take him seriously when he was serious enough for both of them. Plus, she'd had it up to her eyeballs with his attitude. And in front of the books no less.

"Nope. Occupational hazard."

With that, she walked away, not caring if he was pissed at her or not. She could afford to be unapologetically honest with him because she really didn't have anything to lose. Well, except the $80,000 paycheck.

Aurelia moved through the stacks of books, torn between wanting to curl up in one of the dozen or so comfy armchairs littered throughout the space with one and devour it, and seeing what other treasures she might discover. Curiosity won over and she found herself down a dark row of distressed leather books that looked over a century old.

"Wow. These must be ancient," she whispered.

"Over three hundred years old," Philip said behind her. She jumped in spite of herself. This man was constantly surprising her in one way or another. "It's the royal family history since we were a part of Russia until now." His palm sat gentle but firm on her lower back, and small electric pulses emanated from there like an epicenter of pleasure.

"Wow," she whispered.

Philip's hand slid from her back and he turned her around to face him. "Aurelia, can we talk about last night?"

The change in conversation was as jarring as his mood earlier. Her head pounded, a searing pain acting like a knife in the back of her skull as the full weight of what she'd done—sleep with a royal—settled on her shoulders. Guilt robbed her of any joy the library might have given her.

"I'm sorry for that; it was a mistake…"

He waved her off, a weak smile on his face. The pathetic look he cast down on her made her feel cheap, like the clothes she'd brought with her to Aldonia—unfit for a Prince.

"It wasn't. It was a delicious fling and I, um, I enjoyed every minute. But you can see why it would be a problem for both of us if it were to continue."

She did, of course she did. He was so far out of her league it was laughable. She'd even made the same promise to herself before he'd kissed her again in the guest suite. Had she somehow alluded otherwise?

Ugh. This was getting too complicated, but she couldn't afford to mess up her opportunity to pay her dad back after all he'd done to support her after Brian's attack. She'd put the Prince out of her mind once and for all, even if it almost killed her to do it.

She nodded, but words escaped her.

"Good, and thank you for your understanding and discretion. Now, I have an appointment I can't miss. Can you entertain yourself without getting into too much trouble?" It was meant as a joke, but Aurelia felt chastised for something she wasn't sure she'd done. And discretion?

As if a soul would believe her if she proclaimed to have slept with the Prince?

Coolness brushed off Philip as he closed the door to the library behind them, chilling Aurelia despite the near hundred-degree air that wrapped around her like a heavy blanket.

"I'll be fine," she told him, turning her voice as icy as his.

Two could play at this game. Though as soon as she thought the words, she had the feeling that this "game" wasn't really one at all, and that losing could have dire consequences for them both.

As she walked away, she caught him glancing back at her. If she didn't know better, she'd swear he had the same realization.

CHAPTER FOUR: A ROYAL MESS

The light breeze rolling in off the desert smelled of creosote and the hint of salt from the sea to the south, but it did nothing to cool Philip off. He couldn't get the altercation with Aurelia out of his head. Nor could he order his brain to stop reminding him how her long, shapely legs had filled her white, linen pants, leaving very little to his overactive imagination. His fingers itched to trace her legs, her taut stomach, the curve of her breasts. Had he not experienced that exquisite pleasure for himself already, that urge might not be as all-consuming as it was.

Then there was the matter of the way she grated on his every nerve, demanded things of him she had no right to demand. The juxtaposition between her mood and physicality was throwing him off. The former was rough, jagged, and bristly, while the latter was all curves and soft edges. Not a good mix if he was supposed to be forgetting about her.

To that end, what the actual heck had he been thinking asking her to stay, and just after the admonition from Petre?

"Wow, you managed to drive her off and ask her to stick around for a month in the same breath, huh? Tell me again how good you are with the ladies?"

Philip had filled Gregory in on the exchange in the hopes of getting some advice, but he was starting to regret that decision.

"Don't start, Gregory." Philip buried his head in his hands, as defeated as he had been when he'd attempted a negotiation of a trade treaty with the Republic of Georgia. He'd come home from that deal with nothing more than a case of fine wine and a black eye from their guard after a minor miscommunication, despite the fact that his aunt was queen. Every interaction with Aurelia was like that—much of what he wanted to say was lost in translation, even though they both spoke English.

"Ha ha, I'm not getting in the middle of this one. But if she gets to be too much for you, I'll take her off your hands. This one's special. Sexy as hell, too."

The now-familiar urge to protect Aurelia rose up like bile in the back of Philip's throat, and he shot up from his seat. Gregory was a good man, one of the best actually, but Philip abhorred the idea of her with anyone, even his best friend. Especially his best friend. It hit too close to home.

He hoped the look of pure contempt he shot his friend said as much.

"Which is precisely why I don't want you anywhere near her."

Gregory laughed, waved Philip off as if to say he understood.

"Speaking of which, I need you to go to dinner in my place tonight. Tell her the story of how we met, how you became my stand-in. Anything really, just so long as I don't have to see her."

"Why'd you do that? Didn't you just ask her to stay to get an 'exclusive' interview with you?"

Philip ran his hands through his hair. That was just it—he could have offered to give her the story while she was there on assignment, but for some cursed reason he hadn't worked out, he wanted her to stay longer than the week her original contract outlined. Which, of course didn't compute with how absolutely crazy she made him, how half the time he ached to get as far from her as possible.

And then the other half he spent wanting to get as close to her as nature would allow. Preferably with both of them naked.

And therein lay the rub. He wanted her as wholly as he'd ever wanted a woman, and yet couldn't make good on that. She was there to tell his story, and besides, she was a working-class American. Not exactly a good fit for a Prince.

Jesus. This was a mess. A royal effing mess that he'd created. And he couldn't see a way out of it, either.

"I haven't thought any of this through if I'm being honest," Philip admitted to Gregory. "She gets under my skin and I haven't worked out if that's a good or a bad thing yet."

"It sounds good to me. You like her, I can tell. I've seen that look on your face before with—"

Philip threw a hand in the air to stop Gregory before he said another word. The tremor had started up again, but he stymied it by shoving his hands in his pockets.

"Don't you dare say her name. You swore you wouldn't." His expression tightened, and a small muscle twitched in his jaw. Even his voice shook, proof that he wasn't nearly over the... *situation* Gregory referred to. Until he was, he had no business entertaining thoughts about any woman, even one he magnetically felt pulled to like Aurelia.

"Well, anyway, Aurelia's different. Special."

"She's annoying is what she is," Philip grumbled. Though he agreed with Gregory that there was something he couldn't put a finger on—the same something that inspired him to invite her to stay at the castle for a month. A mistake so far as he could tell, but one he couldn't—and wouldn't—take back.

"You don't really believe that or you wouldn't have

asked her to stay."

"I know. And until I figure out how to fix this, I need you to stand in."

Gregory smiled, a look that reminded Philip of their childhood where that smile usually meant fun for them both. And trouble, a whole lot of trouble. "Does that mean I get to wine and dine her?"

Philip shot Gregory another look that doubled as a threat. *Not on his life.* Gregory chuckled, slapped Philip on the knee.

"Fine, I get it. She's taken. Why don't you ask her out, then? When's the last time you went on an actual date? You're getting stale, my friend."

Gregory went to the small ice box in the corner of his suite and procured two Belgian ales. He held one out to Philip, who snatched it without raising his head. He didn't even comment that it was barely two in the afternoon. A beer was definitely needed.

"You know I can't do that."

"Why? Because of what *she* did to you? You've got to let that go. What're you gonna stay single for the rest of your life? I think the reason this woman's getting the best of you is because you're putting up walls. If you just try to relax into it, see where it can go, you might surprise yourself."

"Yes, but where can it go?" Philip asked, taking a long pull from his beer. "She and I are diametrically opposed in every way. I mean, she's American, for starters, and a journalist to top it off. What kind of cosmic joke would it be to fall for the one woman I can't talk to without everything I say being used against my family? My family that avoids journalists and the press like they're the plague, in case you forgot."

Gregory laughed. "Yeah, that does present a problem. But then, you never went for the simple and easy way, did you?" Philip glared at Gregory, whose eyes glinted with mischief. "Well, then take her out of here, show her the countryside. It allows you to be with her where your family isn't the center of conversation and gives her something to write about. They don't call us the jewel of the east for nothing—she'll love it."

Philip mulled over his choices while he took another pull from his beer. His best friend had a point. He'd gotten himself into this mess by inviting her to stay at the castle for a month. If he didn't make good on his offer, she was likely to dig on her own and who knew what she'd discover then. Thank God the King and Queen were out of the country the next two months while he parsed through this dumpster fire of a situation.

"All right, but you and I need to get on the same page when it comes to what to say to her if she gets, you know, journalist-y."

"Have you thought about the truth? She's gonna find out sooner or later anyway."

"I can't go there—not without running it by the rest of the family first," Philip said, though that was his first inclination as well. "There's more at stake here than just my issues."

Like a small nation of people.

"She already knows the most damning part. Why not share the rest? Your brother will understand."

"Not yet. But let's say I take you up on a trip. Where should I take her?"

"How about wine country? That never fails."

"Sure, for a floozy I want to sleep with on the first date."

"Didn't you already sleep with Aurelia? That cat's out of the bag, my friend. Besides, it's not like that's not going to happen again. I've seen the way you look at her. It's like she's a piece of meat and you've been on a desert island with nothing but nuts for a year."

Philip snapped his fingers, ignoring the question that had plagued him as well. "That's it. I'll take her to Lapochka Island. My mother's family is from there and the castle grounds still exist."

Heels echoed down the stone hallway. Philip lowered his voice as they neared. Despite his less-than-optimistic outlook on the journalist and the story she came for, a twinge of excitement fluttered around in his chest like an anxious bird wanting to escape. He was actually looking forward to the idea of a trip. How long had it been since he'd traveled for pleasure, without the burden of the crown behind him?

An image of his parents on the shore of the Black Sea, Philip and his brother splashing around at their feet, flashed across his vision, interrupting his thoughts. He must have been eight? Nine years old? That was the last year Robert had been home with them, the last year before he'd been forced to take over the family business. The last year his parents had been alive. Aside from the ache that filled his chest at the memory, he had to admit the beach was where he'd spent his last happy moments.

"We'll stay at the old beach house—it's nothing like the castle, but I love it there." The vision of his parents dissipated, forced from his mind as he pictured Aurelia there with him. Aurelia in a bathing suit. His cheeks flushed hot and his pants tightened around the waist. "I have a feeling she will, too. Thanks for taking care of the homefront while I'm away."

"Gotta put this outfit to use somehow. Enjoy yourself." They clinked glasses, and Gregory set his on the table. "Empty. I'm gonna grab another. You want one?" Philip nodded as Gregory stepped out of the room.

Just as Philip took the last pull of his beer, Aurelia came around the corner, her nose buried in a map, a glass of wine balancing a small plate of cheese atop it. She knocked into the console table in the front of the room, tipping over Gregory's empty bottle and a candle holder that was older than the castle in the process. The noise that bounced off the walls of the large room was deafening.

"Oh, shoot!" she muttered, putting down the map and

food to clean up the inadvertent mess she'd made. She had no clue where she was, that much was evident in the way she took her time moving around the room on all fours. He chuckled, then opted to give her a hand.

As he made his way to her, Philip relished in the brief moment of anonymity where she hadn't seen him yet. He couldn't take his eyes off her rolling curves. She still wore her white linen top and pants, the latter snug against her tight backside that was on full display for him. Her hair was pulled up in a messy bun, and when she turned on her knees, eyes still pinned to the ground, he noticed a few curly tendrils that had sprung loose framed her face. She pursed her lips to blow one back, but it fell right back in front of her eyes. She huffed in frustration, but Philip's fingers itched to tuck each of the errant strands behind the soft skin of her earlobe. Her cheeks were flushed pink from the heat that radiated in from the desert beyond the walls. The itch in his fingers shifted to the image of another way he could flush Aurelia's cheeks if she'd let him. With her in the same position she was in now.

"Lost?" he asked her, guilt at admiring her physique without her consent or knowledge finally getting the best of him.

Aurelia's head shot up at the sound of his voice, and her gaze landed on Philip, who was mere feet from her. Her eyes registered veiled confusion until she took in the room she found herself in. Then the look shifted to embarrassment, finally settling on annoyance when she seemed to realize he'd been staring at her. To add insult to injury, he didn't turn away. He couldn't—not when her gaze pulled him in as if he were tethered by a thin rope to her long lashes.

He wanted to apologize, his mouth open, the words sliding past his throat that was now inexplicably dry as the desert when she stood up and brushed her pants off. He bristled, but bit his lip to keep from shooting off something curt. He'd been the one caught staring.

"I'm sorry, Your Grace," she said. Her cheeks went from pink to cherry red, and her voice quivered with embarrassment. "I was just trying to figure out how to get back to the gardens. The chef gave me some cheese and wine and I thought I'd type some of my notes on the royal history before dinner. That is, if dinner is still on, Your Highness." She spoke those two words like they caused her pain to utter them.

Philip stood there, still as stone, the rebuttal stinging his pride, his heart. He didn't think anyone had ever flat-out refused to give his position the respect it demanded as she did.

"Of course it's still on. Though plans have changed ever so slightly."

"And how's that? You know, just because I'm sticking around, it doesn't mean you can expect me to go along with whatever you drum up by way of distracting me. I'd appreciate some notice about our plans in advance so I can plan," she spat out, her bottom lip quivering with what looked like rage. Directed at him. She really did hate him, didn't she? Well, what else could he have done except tell her their affair was a bad idea? She had to see the million reasons it was. Except all he saw in her gaze was fire and wrath.

God, he wished that the flames in her eyes didn't turn him on. It was rather humiliating to be standing there, half hard, while the woman responsible for that glared at him as if she wanted him to evaporate on the spot.

He had every damn right to ask her to go along with his last-minute plans. She was his employee for the next month. Still, he was determined not to prove her right and act like the jerk she believed him to be. It was a Herculean effort in futility, sure, but it was worth a shot.

"I'm terribly sorry. But I think you'll forgive me when you see where we're going."

"We?" she asked, her arms crossed.

Don't stare at her chest. His gaze dipped down despite his mind arguing that was a horrible idea. He tried not to notice this gesture of hers pushed her ample breasts up so they peeked out of her white blouse. He especially tried not to picture what they would look like if he tore that shirt off.

"Yes. You and I. We're going to a private royal beach. I'd pack a swimsuit, because the water there is as near heaven as I'd ever like to come." When she didn't respond, he continued. "Do you have any food preferences? The chef will need a list of your desires for the rest of the week. Oh, and we will leave tomorrow afternoon." He calmed the slight tremor in his hands by shoving his hands in his pockets. Her gaze sharpened, but she sighed.

"Fine. With respect to foods, I have no allergies, and I'm not very picky. Whatever you suggest will be sufficient. Now, will I be able to use what we discuss in the story? I'd rather not take the time from the castle grounds, but if you could answer some of my questions, the trip won't be a total loss," she said.

Philip bit down on the side of his cheek so he didn't blurt out the response that came to mind. If she thought he was rude before...

"You may use everything we discuss, Ms. Beck. Now, you should prepare for our trip, but I look forward to spending time with you."

Surprisingly, as soon as he uttered the words, an empty ache from a cavernous part of his chest argued that it was true. He wanted Aurelia's body, and though her tongue was as sharp as her mind, he couldn't deny that she intrigued him. Maybe this trip wouldn't be the loss she thought it would be—if he handled it right, that was. He'd simply do his best to make it memorable for her and hope that was enough to soften her attitude toward him.

If not, it was going to be an excruciatingly long month.

Gregory came around the corner then, his trademarked mischievous smile tugging at the corners of his mouth. So, he'd heard their exchange, had he? He was probably loving that Philip was taken to task by this aggravating woman. No doubt Gregory thought Philip deserved the dressing down. That didn't bother him near as much as seeing Aurelia's face light up when she noticed Gregory, though.

Jealousy ate at his lungs, stole his breath.

"I have a bone to pick with you," she said, playfully slugging Gregory on the shoulder. The jealousy in Philip's chest roared and doubled its efforts to snatch any hint of life from Philip. His chest burned.

"Yes, I see that. I'm sorry I lied to you. But you get it now, don't you?" Gregory shrugged his shoulders, his smile brighter than ever. How did he pull off that nonchalance?

She didn't look at Philip but nudged her chin in his direction. He felt the slight as a stark dismissal, not the first from her.

"I don't, not fully anyway. But I'll get there."

"Still, I apologize. Have fun this weekend. You'll love the beach he's taking you to."

"We'll see. Can we do lunch when I'm back? I'll have some questions for you now that I know who you are." She winked and smiled at Gregory. Anger constricted Philip's heart. When she wrapped her arms around his friend in a hug that could be read as more than just friendly, Philip almost bit through the side of his cheek.

Why was it so easy for Gregory? It wasn't just his laid-back demeanor, either. He'd had a way of making friends with women—and taking that friendship to the bedroom in record time—before he ever wore the crown.

Philip, on the other hand, slept with women, sure, but he couldn't talk to them the way Gregory could. Not to mention the fact that this particular woman called him out on issues with his country, with the way he ran it, as well as his personality. She had him even more tongue-tied than the rest. Yet, somehow, she was all he could think about since her arrival.

She didn't say anything to Philip on her way out, just

tossed him a curt wave before she turned the corner again with her wine and cheese. As soon as she was out of sight, Gregory closed the door and laughed, a guffaw that filled the amphitheater space resonating off the walls.

Philip could only groan.

"You've got it bad, brother."

"I don't know what I have, but it feels terminal."

"Yeah, and she's not having any of it, is she?"

"You saw that, too, huh? And by the way, you weren't very helpful when it came to having my back." Philip slugged Gregory on the shoulder as he walked over to the small fridge and helped himself to another beer without bothering to procure one for his friend.

"She wasn't wrong, Philip. You're tough. It's why you're good at your job—perfect, even—but it's Hell when it comes to dating. You've got to loosen up, learn to have fun."

Philip nodded and took a long pull from his bottle before setting it down at his feet. He ran his hands through his hair, thinking about the ways he could spoil Aurelia this trip, show her a good time. Money certainly wouldn't be an issue. Ideas started flowing quicker than he could catalogue them.

"Okay. I can do that."

"I'm not so sure, but I'll enjoy watching you try."

"I've got my work cut out for me, don't I?"

Gregory laughed, covered the short distance to the fridge, and got himself a drink. "You do, friend, you really do. I'd start with making an actual plan, because the one you came up with earlier was absolute crap."

Philip downed his ale in one long swig, appreciating the way the alcohol cooled him from the center out. A deep-seated desire to please Aurelia emanated from the same place the jealousy had sprung from, and was as unexpected. He'd give Aurelia the best month she could have because all of a sudden, that mattered more than anything—more than the secret he'd been carrying for three years now, more than what his family thought. If for no other reason than to turn her opinion of him, he needed to do this.

As he made his way to the royal wine cellars to pick out three or four rare bottles for their trip, he cataloged every romantic, spoiling gesture he could think of. Sure, this contract with Aurelia was a business agreement, but maybe, for the first time in his life, he'd be able to mix business with a little pleasure.

CHAPTER FIVE: ROYAL PERKS

Aurelia drew in a slow breath of appreciation and awe. She'd imagined they'd be taking a government plane to the beach—some property that had been in the royal family for six generations—but she wasn't remotely prepared for the extravagant opulence of the jet.

The seats were off-white leather—the same color as the walls in her apartment but much richer in tone, and the floors were hardwood. *Hard wood.* On an airplane. There were flat-screen televisions big enough to draw a good bar crowd on a Sunday night at each seat, and that wasn't taking into account the one that was placed center stage. It was a freaking mini theater.

She exhaled as slowly as she'd breathed in, the magnitude of what she'd agreed to hitting her with the force of a semi. This was some next-level traveling. But then again, the man traveling with her was beyond in his own right. A shudder of what her body had experienced the night she'd arrived at the mercy of his hands, his lips, his body rippled down her spine. A heat that had nothing to do with embarrassment radiated through her veins, settling in the apex between her thighs, making her damp and wholly uncomfortable. She'd tried to play it cool the day before, to pretend he hadn't affected her so viscerally, but later in the day, he'd raked his gaze over her when she'd unwittingly meandered into his suite, reigniting those feelings. Knowing he was behind her now, she could feel his gaze rolling over her, making it impossible to put their tryst from her mind.

He'd meant what he said about not continuing their affair, and for the most part, she agreed with him. Philip annoyed the ever-loving crap out of her, and he was caustic and ran his country like a dictator.

But for some inexplicable reason, in spite of the relationship with Brian when she'd narrowly escaped with her life, despite the world of experience between her and Philip, she couldn't deny the sparks between her and the Prince.

Damn him for having a hold on her that in no way made her feel good about being alone in the confined, airborne space with him for the next few hours. She couldn't even think about the next few days without her heart threatening to pound through her ribcage.

As if she'd conjured him with her explicit thoughts, Philip came up behind her, placed one hand firmly on her hip, and reached around her waist with a glass of red wine. Fortunately, from his vantage point, he couldn't see how her bottom lip trembled as a result of the hand that gripped her waist. How was she supposed to sip what she assumed was a stellar glass of wine when she couldn't control her faculties?

God, how she wanted to chug the liquid, bolster the courage she desperately needed to find if she planned on surviving this week. If only she could breathe. Stirrings of lust built in her chest, then wasted no time racing south between her legs.

She was suddenly hyper-aware of the thong underwear she'd worn that morning as Philip's thumb rested on the band. She tried to focus on the glass in her hand, the music playing in the background so her pulse could regulate, though that was near impossible every time she was around Philip. A beat of relief came when he left to procure his own glass, and she could finally inhale, concentrate again. When he wasn't so close to her, she wanted to strangle him, but the opposite occurred when he came within a foot of her. Jesus.

She inhaled the floral bouquet of the wine, impressed by the aroma and the vintage it implied. But then, of course she would be. She hadn't stopped being impressed since she'd touched down in Aldonia.

The Waterford crystal goblet she held was only one example of the small, yet exquisite accents in the private cabin, adding to her growing sense of awe. Hardwood countertops matched the floors, and a full bar with only high-end liquors and liqueurs lined a whole wall of the place. Silver cutlery and china table settings accentuated the fact that this plane was meant for royalty.

It was, of course, staffed by a woman who could have passed as a Norwegian princess she was so stunning, so regal. Instead of the usual flight attendant uniform, the tall blonde wore linen pants that came down over open-toed stilettos and a gold knit tank that showed off tan, fit arms.

She smiled pleasantly at Aurelia, but her eyes wandered to Philip, her smile shifting to a more formal greeting. He offered a simple nod at the woman, who curtsied before busying herself plating an elegant-looking meal of salmon and rice pilaf. The power belied in this simple exchange sent waves of discomfort rolling over Aurelia. With the snap of his fingers, Philip controlled a staff, a country, something that wasn't at all in Aurelia's wheelhouse. She no more knew how to interact with royalty than she desired to. Yet, she also couldn't stop the growing attraction for Philip if she tried. It left her feeling at odds with herself as the plane moved toward the runway.

Before she could give that line of thinking too much weight, Philip's hand was back on her hip. She could have flown to the southern tip of the country herself with all the electricity surging between his skin and the thin veil of fabric shielding hers. He sizzled, branded her with his touch. Left her craving more.

"Cheers," he said, his voice low and sensual. She shuddered in the chill of the air conditioning that blasted her from behind, ruffling her hair over her shoulders.

"Cheers." She took one sip and broke out in a grin. She'd had nothing but good wine since she got there, but this took it to a bougie, almost sinful level. "This is incredible."

"I should hope so. It's a 1967 vintage from the royal vineyard. Grenache and Petite Verdot. There's just this bottle left."

Aurelia almost spit out what was in her mouth, which, of course, would have been a cardinal sin, damning her to a lifetime of drinking only Boone's Farm.

"You're kidding." When he shook his head as if to say *what's the big deal?* she sipped slower, appreciating what no one else would ever be able to. Still, it flung into sharp relief the difference between their lifestyles. She'd better get used to that disparity if she had any hope of surviving the month in Aldonia.

"Why me?" she asked, swiping her hand from the wine to the cabin behind her, glittering in the soft afternoon light.

It was the one question that had plagued her every moment since he'd made the offer for her to stay.

He regarded her carefully, eyes on her lips as he licked his own. She watched him measure his response, choosing each word carefully. He was the most reticent person she'd ever met, but as the most important man in his country, she imagined freedom of thought, of speech, was a job liability. What might it take to strip him of that resolve?

Strip him bare. She shivered.

"You deserve it. I asked you to stay, and I want you to enjoy your time here, not just treat it like work."

She considered that for a moment before she offered a

response. Could she do that—really relax here, put her journalistic instincts to bed and indulge? She wouldn't know where to begin. Everything was budgeted so closely—her time, her finances, her fun—that she didn't think she could let loose without some serious indulging in alcohol first. First-class wine like this might help nudge that along.

"Thank you," she said, sincerely. Her voice was low, husky, and she thought she heard Philip's breath hitch in his chest.

"You're welcome." He put his hand on her knee and gestured out of the window. Her skin screamed with electricity, like every other square inch of her that he'd touched. Why the heck did she think a short sundress would be the professional choice? If only the darned castle wasn't in the middle of a freaking desert, the day wasn't hot enough to melt her phone cover when she'd left it outside for a moment.

With Philip's skin directly on hers, she was without a barrier to protect the self-control that waned with each minute she spent near him. Sure, she was attracted to him, physically at least, but she hadn't been intimate with anyone since Brian and already guilt ripped at her chest for breaking her self-imposed year of chastity to recover from that relationship. So, she clamped her legs together, the ache between her legs pulsing.

"Look at the mountain range to the north. I'd love to take you there on the way home if you're interested. There's spectacular hiking and crystal-green waterfalls that would make Hawaii envious."

Aurelia looked out over the expanse below her, grateful for the distraction. The tan and brown land—not as breathtaking from above as it was when one stood in the rolling hills that teemed with wildflowers and other signs of desert life—undulated until the hills rose to massive peaks that took her breath away.

"Is that still in Aldonia?"

"It is. It's the natural border between us and Azerbaijan."

"They're beautiful, but there's snow. I didn't bring anything even resembling hiking gear with me, especially not cold-weather hiking gear. I'm sorry; I'd really love to explore them."

She would, too. She loved hiking in the Adirondacks and Poconos every chance she got in the summers, but she was most definitely not prepared for anything like that this trip. If her freaking sundress was any indication.

"Don't be. We'll go shopping and make sure you have what you need. Trust me, you don't want to miss this. Persian leopards have been sighted the past month, a rare treasure this far north."

"Are you sure I'll need gear to see them? I'd hate to spend money on something I've got copies of back home. Even with your generous paycheck for this assignment, I want to be a little frugal. The money could help me make a significant dent in my debt."

She hated talking about money with a man who looked as if he was made of it. Would he even comprehend a fraction of what she'd had to do to get back on her feet after a divorce and the crippling debt it saddled her with?

Philip took both her hands in his. Heat pooled in her belly when his thumb ran circles over her palms. Why couldn't he be an overweight, end-of-his-prime prince? Balding would help, too.

"Let's get one thing straight. You aren't to worry about money while you're here. Your money won't be accepted even if you do. If I want to take you hiking, I will buy you what you'll need. You can take it home with you when you leave, or donate it if you'd care to. But we won't have this discussion again. When I ask if you'd like to do something, simply answer yes or no, but the cost had better not cross your mind. Is that understood?"

Aurelia wanted to slap him for speaking to her like she was a member of his staff. Maybe he could get away with that with his guards, his housekeepers, but her? Not a chance. However, there was a small voice in the back of her head that silenced the larger part of her that ached to tell him off.

Let him, it said. *He's right—you deserve it, and this is a once-in-a-lifetime opportunity. You're a real-life Cinderella.*

She was, too. For a month, at least. The thought warmed her skin despite the cool air that fell on her exposed shoulders.

If only Philip was the prince you got to kiss at the end of it all. At the end of the aisle.

She tried not to think too long on that. Philip was most definitely kissable. Plus some, as their unexpected and unrepeatable encounter proved. But the way his eyes shifted from clear and sunny, as bright a green-blue as she'd ever seen, to dark and stormy, more gray than any other color, meant danger lay there as well. She had to be cautious, aware at all times where he was concerned.

Besides, why was she even daydreaming about marriage when she'd just gained her freedom from a wreck of a union? Even courting the idea with someone as hot and cold as Philip was dangerous.

"Okay. I agree. And I'd love to see the mountains. What are they called?" She settled into his brief but fascinating description of the land they flew over, surprised by how expansive Aldonia was. On the map, it had appeared no bigger than her city and its five boroughs. But now, flying over the swathe of desert flanked by majestic peaks on one side and by a deep-blue body of water that was just coming into view on the other, Aurelia's breath hitched in her chest. It was gorgeous.

The rest of the flight passed with her and Philip in easy conversation about Aldonia, about America's new president, and how she was faring. It was nice, albeit a bit unnerving considering their previous interactions at the castle. Philip was different than he was at the palace, where it seemed he had the weight of the world on his shoulders.

Here, he relaxed into his leather seat, his feet crossed but propped up on a small stool, his arms languid. He was at home, in his element.

Her fingers itched to dig out her pen and pad to scribble herself a reminder to come back to this while they were away. This sort of living—the royal responsibility and rewards—seemed so well-suited to Philip that it made her wonder why he'd given any of it up, even temporarily.

She didn't want to go there just then, though. She enjoyed his company, and it felt good simply to sit back and enjoy the surprisingly best conversation she'd had in a while, especially without a notepad in her hand.

For the first time in months, years even, work slipped to the back of her mind.

As they disembarked from the plane, Aurelia breathed in deeply. Salt and sulfur flooded her senses, almost bowling her over with the images it called up from her past.

It had been over three years since she'd been to the beach—since her mother had passed. The heaviness of the damp, salty air weighed on her shoulders now, like anvils preventing her from moving forward. When she'd agreed to come with Philip, she hadn't considered the possibility of a surprise assault of memories. Each one hurt worse than the last.

Her mother leading her down to the water's edge, both of them squealing when a rogue wave chased them back up the shore.

Her mother teaching her how to swim in the light chop when she was seven, pulling her out of the water when Aurelia had swallowed too much.

The shells her mother sent her when she was in college and too busy to make the annual summer trip to Avalon. What she wouldn't give to go back, to leave the books at home, to have just one more memory with her mother by the sea.

Aurelia stepped into the car that awaited them on the

tarmac and made the drive in silence, her hands shaking. She barely registered the champagne on ice and large, flat-screen TV the sedan boasted, and certainly didn't appreciate the lavish details like she had on the plane.

"Are you cold?" Philip asked. His hand found hers and squeezed it.

She shook her head no. The trembling in her arms that had now spread to her core had nothing to do with the temperature.

"Are you okay, Aurelia?"

She nodded, unable to speak with the lump that had unexpectedly built in her throat. She attempted a smile, but it never made its way to her eyes. The car stopped, and she got out, Philip refusing to let go of her grasp.

"Talk to me," he urged, rubbing her palm affectionately. "Something happened between the plane and now. What is it?"

She faltered—Philip being kind and supportive, the sun brandishing its mark on her shoulders, the briny scent of salty air—all of it was too much for her to take in at once. Her eyes filled with the same salty moisture that coiled around her with the breeze.

"I'm fine," she said, her voice barely more than a whisper. She shut her eyes, a rogue tear slipping down her cheek. Philip brushed it with the pad of his thumb. "I just haven't been to the beach in a while. It holds a lot of memories for me."

With that, another flash of her mother picking her up and twirling her, the sea breeze blowing her long, red hair in waves of its own, came blindingly to the back of Aurelia's closed lids.

Only Philip's hand in hers kept her grounded to the present when she so desperately wanted to dissolve into her mother's arms. Aurelia would never walk the sandy shore collecting wave-worn shells with her mother, the thought of which hit her with the force of a hurricane.

Her knees buckled, but Philip's arm was around her in

a flash, steadying her.

"I'm not going anywhere. I've got you," he said.

She nodded, her breath still.

"Come with me. There's something I want you to see." He led her forward along a path lined with bougainvillea and crushed shells. Aurelia let herself be pulled along for the walk, unsure she could have resisted even if she wanted to.

They walked for close to five minutes, neither of them saying a word except for the frustrated grumbles Philip made each time a bush scratched his arm. She was about to comment on the fact that their path was disintegrating when he moved the branches from in front of her to reveal a pristine cove with the whitest sand she'd ever seen. The water in front of her was tranquil, turquoise almost the color of Philip's eyes, but beyond a small reef border, whitecaps dominated the sea, a deep blue-gray.

It was a perfect metaphor for the Philip she had come to know—tranquil and inviting at one end, fierce and mercurial at the other.

"Where are we?" she asked. It was only then she registered the fact that she'd allowed this stranger—a royal stranger, but a man she'd known less than a week nonetheless—to take her to an undisclosed location and she hadn't thought to text her father, Lily, or anyone for that matter. Still, none of her trusty sixth-sense alarms went off. Instead, looking out over the water that glittered under the fierce glare of the sun, a wave of calm washed over her.

"The Black Sea."

"It's the most beautiful beach I've ever seen." And it was. She'd never been anywhere near there, but still, something was familiar about the beach.

"Thank you. I'm glad you like it. It's ours for the week. Yours, rather." He looked up and behind them.

She followed his gaze to an impressively large, but tasteful home with a whitewashed wrap-around deck that stood proud atop a hill above them. Then she looked back at Philip, at the way the sea was put to shame by his eyes— more crystal than organic material—and without giving any thought to the consequences, stepped up on her toes, wrapped her arms around his neck, and pressed her lips to his.

The connection was instant. A groan passed between their breaths. Aurelia was unsure of who let it loose, only that it ignited them both.

She parted her lips for him, inviting him in, tasting an intoxicating blend of coffee and the salt that hung heavy in the air as his tongue tangled with hers. His hands slid down her backside, lifting the fabric of her sundress and cupping her cheeks.

It might be the worst idea she'd ever had, but when the softness of his perfect lips enveloped her grief, her pain, her overworked body, she didn't care. She never wanted to leave where she was in that perfect moment, wrapped up in a man's arms and lips that were starting to feel better every second.

KRISTINE LYNN

CHAPTER SIX: ROYAL MISTAKE

Philip's ability to think slowed to a glacial pace as Aurelia's arms wrapped around his neck and pulled him down to her. Then, a surge of electricity, followed by blackness, short-circuited his brain when her lips made contact.

Jesus. Heat radiated throughout his entire body that had absolutely nothing to do with the warm breeze blowing in off the sea.

He'd been kissed by more attractive women than he could remember, many of them impressive lovers who knew their way around the pleasures of a man. But never—*never*—had such a spark of recognition, of desire, flooded his system like it did as Aurelia's lips parted, her tongue teasing his, inviting him inside her mouth. If he thought their previous night together was hot, it was nothing compared to this kiss that grew in intimacy as it deepened.

Philip growled as she moved closer, her breasts pressed against his chest. He was hard under his slacks. As his hands moved over her sides, he memorized her curves the way he had the winding mountain passes by his brother's castle in his Porsche. He appreciated the way one led to another, each more dangerous than the last. A shudder coursed through him as his hands brushed the underside of her breasts.

No bra.

Want and need took over, but just as his hands slid south of her hips to her perfect backside, she pulled away, her lips swollen and wet. She bit her bottom lip and ran a hand through her long, brown hair that was pulled over her right shoulder. In this light, red highlights glittered amongst the auburn curls that the sea had turned feral, luminous, and wild.

She was *beautiful.* The most classically beautiful woman he'd laid eyes on. The acknowledgment of this shook him more than the kiss itself. Before that moment, she'd just been the annoying reporter pestering him for a story, the sexual mistake he'd made.

But now…

"I'm sorry," she said, an embarrassed smile pulling at the corners of her mouth that had been on his just moments earlier. "I know you said we shouldn't do that anymore, but I couldn't help it."

"Don't be. Unless you plan on keeping those lips from mine. Then you can be filled with remorse. I'm sorry I ever said we should stop." The swelling against his zipper echoed that sentiment.

She giggled, a sound more harmonic than the small waves that lapped at their feet.

"I don't want to stop, either. I mean, not yet, but you have a way of pulling regrets from me like my ex. I just think we should slow down a little."

Philip cringed at the mention of an ex. The idea that anyone else had kissed those lips, touched those curves, lit a fire in his center that was all rage. He tampered it by remembering how nice it was to hold her, to not have to spar with her verbal jabs, and instead use her mouth in a way that suited them both much better.

"Yes, well, should we settle in and grab a cocktail?"

"We really get to stay here all week?"

He nodded and smiled. He'd done a good job in choosing this location. It was so well-suited to her tastes, tastes he was only just discovering. And God, how he wanted to find out more, find out everything about her. Another surprising revelation.

"Do we need to go back and grab the bags?"

"They're already at the house in our rooms. I gave you the suite with the deck facing the water on the first floor since it has stairs leading down here. If you'd rather switch, let me know."

She squealed with delight. Her soft curls bounced when she jumped and clapped her hands. Philip laughed. Aurelia was a different woman here already. More relaxed. Less of an edge.

"C'mon. The chef will have appetizers ready."

He followed her up the stairs that led to the master suite, trying and failing not to stare at the perfect, round backside that peeked from underneath Aurelia's sundress. He caught a glimpse of pink lace and his heart rate raced as if he'd sprinted up the stairs.

This woman...

Philip opened the door to the room and smiled at Aurelia's sharp intake of breath behind him. He placed a hand on her hip, a rush of heat pooling in his stomach as her hand covered his.

"Do you like it?" he whispered in her ear.

God, he wanted her to love it. He brushed his lips over her neck, and she purred. Her hand was at her mouth, her bottom lip delicately worried by perfectly white teeth. Desire to bring her mouth to his and let his teeth take over pounded against his chest. When she nodded, he smiled with relief.

"This is too much, Philip. Do you have anything smaller, less...I don't know, *fancy*?"

Fancy? He glanced around the room at the stained glass of the beachside that served as a wall with the shower behind it, at the bed with its white down comforter and light wood posts, at the small bar in the corner with an attached seating room. He tried to envision it through her eyes but could only see the place he came each summer with his parents—a place that started to feel claustrophobic with four people all crowded in the same five-thousand square feet. The idea that she found this humble cottage fancy endeared her to him. It was so opposite to what he was used to from the women he'd been with before. His money and power had never seemed enough. He'd never been enough for them.

He shook his head. That didn't matter now. Not with Aurelia by his side.

"Why don't I give you a tour and you can decide after that how you feel?"

She nodded again and took the hand he offered. The loss of her body against his was like missing a phantom limb. That kiss had imprinted her to him and he wanted more.

All of her.

But her hand would have to do. For now, anyway.

He took her through the bottom level, doling out a memory or two about each room, careful to leave his private past from the conversation as much as possible. He wanted to share more of who *he* was, where he came from, with Aurelia, but needed to wait for the right time, the right place. Maybe that was there, at the beach house, but they'd just arrived. Besides, he was still reeling from her lips on his, stuck on what it meant to her, what it meant to him.

That, and he wasn't over *her*, she-who-wouldn't-be-named. He wasn't sure he ever would be, but did that mean he didn't ever get to be happy? Aurelia was only staying with him for a month, so perhaps she could be a bridge between what had come before and nearly killed him, and his future.

Perhaps. Only time would give him any answers.

They ended up in the third-floor kitchen, a space that opened up to an impressive patio overlooking not only the cove, but the sea beyond it. Philip retrieved the two glasses of white wine that were set out for them and handed one to Aurelia.

"To you, my guest. I hope this trip will be everything you need."

"To the story, to sharing Aldonia with the world."

Philip put on his most political smile since he couldn't muster up an authentic one. Apparently, the Aurelia he'd gotten to know at the castle was still in there somewhere. What exactly was the story? He'd been trying to work that out since he met Aurelia, since he'd asked her to stay.

"If you don't mind, I'd love to clean up a bit before dinner. Do you mind if I take this to my room?"

"Not at all. You'll take the suite?"

Aurelia grinned, her cheeks rosy, her eyes bright. "I will. I figure when in Aldonia…"

Philip laughed, an altogether rare sensation for him. It erased the hitch in the afternoon brought on by the reminder of why they were there. Her job.

"Live like a royal," he added.

She shook her head, laughter echoing down the hall she disappeared down.

As soon as she was out sight, Philip called over the head of house staff, Lorence. He whispered something, brought out a package, and with a deep bow, Lorence was off with it tucked under his arm. Philip sat alone on the couch, a smile on his face as he sipped his wine.

Fifteen minutes later, Aurelia came out in a white, floor-length cotton shift that—just as Philip suspected—hugged her curves in all the right spots.

"What is this?" she asked, gesturing to the dress. Her voice was laced with annoyance, but a smile betrayed her excitement.

Philip stood and walked to her, gesturing with his finger that she spin and give him a better view. She did, arms outstretched like a windmill. A swoon-worthy windmill that he preferred to see bare.

"A gift. It's made locally, and you'll never wear anything more comfortable. Or so I'm told."

"You've got to stop trying to buy me with presents. I like your company, but I'm here for work. Simple as that."

"So, should I take it back?" he asked, sliding his finger in the strap and trailing it along her collarbone. Her short, halted breath was matched by the flushing of her skin where his hand had been.

He gazed into her dark-brown eyes, marveled at the hints of gold flecked in them. If only she wasn't who she was, he wasn't who he was. Maybe if circumstances were different, he'd kiss her again, and this time, let it go where it would. God knew his whole body pushed him toward her, toward the need she'd ignited in him when she kissed him the first time in his palace.

Aurelia's hands moved over the fabric. Philip didn't even try to hide the way his gaze locked on to her hands, followed them down her body. He licked his lips, desire building in his abdomen, and definitely south of that.

"No. You're right. It's extremely cozy. Thank you."

Philip nodded.

"So, what's on your agenda this week?"

"I thought you made the plans and I just followed along."

"Well, what would you like to do?"

"Honestly? Walk the beach, write, drink more of this fabulous wine. Please tell me it isn't another rare bottle. I'll start to feel guilty that I'm drinking my food budget for the month with each glass."

Philip chuckled. "Not this one. You can find this at a popular vineyard in Georgia."

"The country?"

"Of course. I'm not sure the state has a refined palate when it comes to viniculture. On that note, would you like to tour the royal vineyards?" A list of places he wanted to take her sprang to mind, but it would take a year to cover them all. Oh, what he would do if he had a year with this woman.

Or what she would do to him.

"Would I? Does the Pope wear a red hat?"

"I'm not sure of the relevance of that, but I'll arrange it. For now, let's eat. Would the dining table on the patio suffice?"

"It would. And I have one more request, Philip."

She'd stopped referring to him as Prince Philip at some point. When, he wasn't completely sure. But he didn't care. The sound of his name on her lips more than made up for the formality.

"Name anything. It's yours." He stood a breath away from Aurelia, her mouth close enough to touch without moving his body. He breathed in her scent, floral and sweet, and committed it to memory.

"I want you to enjoy this trip, too. Lighten up. There's plenty of time to use words like *suffice* and *royal duty* when you're back at work. Right now, it's just us and I want to relax, which I can't do if you're acting like a prince all week."

She reached up and took his bottom lip in her mouth, using her teeth to tease him open for her. Her tongue darted in and found his. His heart slammed against his chest when she traced the lip she'd been nibbling on.

He groaned against her, wanting more than the morsel she offered him before pulling away.

Breathless from the second kiss that had him reeling, Philip thought about that. About acting like someone he wasn't, about how convoluted it all was now that Aurelia was there with him, kissing him left and right.

He wished it were as easy as shedding a skin and walking away different, but the levels of confusion wrapped around who he was, who he wanted to be, were so inextricably tied together, it would be impossible. But he could give her a version of the self he wished he was.

He could relax his guard and let her in.

The problem was, what would happen to him, to the kingdom, when he did?

CHAPTER SEVEN: ROYAL PRESENTS

Aurelia awoke on her last day at the beach house a different person. Or, at the very least, a sexually satisfied one. As it turned out, making the first move to kiss him again—this time while he was separated from his royal duties—was the best decision she'd ever made when it came to choosing a lover. He explored her with expert attentiveness, to the point it was as if he could read her mind. He touched her in places she longed for his lips, his hands, to roam without her having to say a word.

She closed her eyes and recalled the night before.

He'd started by nibbling at her neck...

Then worked his way along her collarbone, peppering it with kisses...

Finally trailing his tongue down her side...

And, oh, how she'd squirmed when his mouth found her opening, wet and swollen, how he'd used his tongue to bring her to climax before sliding inside her, his shaft hard and filling her in places she hadn't known existed. Each thrust inside her reminded her body what it could feel at the mercy of an expert lover. She'd come three times—

three times!—before falling asleep, sated and exhausted.

Yet, as she lay there in the satin sheets that still smelled like the salty air mixed with Philip's cinnamon musk, she wondered what it all meant.

Her past—her mother's death and her less-than-pleasant divorce—was kissed away each day by the most handsome man she had ever met, but for some reason, she couldn't completely let go. Philip knew how to make her body succumb to his, how to forget her worries in a bottle of incredible wine or in his hands, sometimes both. But he was holding something back on the emotional front, which made it impossible for her to fully let go either. That, and his lifestyle, fun and exciting as a guest, wasn't anything she could live with long-term. Always being waited on, always watching as those in his country lived without while she drank thousand-dollar bottles of wine, left her wishing for home and the simplicities it offered.

And yet…

The crappy thing was, they wouldn't have time to make this more than just the body-rocking affair it had been the past week even if she wanted it. Already, the strain of the clock taunted her since a week had passed—leaving her seven days closer to going home. To leaving Philip.

She no longer looked forward to the latter like she had when she first met him. His lifestyle, yes, but not the man himself.

She sighed, and, deciding to let him sleep, tiptoed to the shower. Her skin missed the proximity to his almost instantly. She made the water as close to scalding as she could get it and stepped in. The heat penetrated muscles that had been overworked as she came up with inventive ways to show Philip how much her body appreciated and craved his. The steam enveloped her, softening her skin and thoughts.

Just as she was about to leave the comfort of the shower, the door opened and Philip strode in, clad only in his boxer briefs. One look at his bare chest, and her calm dissolved, replaced by memories of his slick chest wet against her naked body, his pelvis against her abdomen, which she could see from the way he stood at half-mast had crossed his mind as well. Damn. She needed to find a way to look past how this man made her feel if she ever wanted to get the story she'd agreed to stay for.

For a fleeting second, Aurelia imagined the worst. What if that was exactly his point? What if that was why he plied her with drinks, with sex, with gifts? So that she'd forget the story altogether?

"Well, hello there, beautiful. I was wondering where you'd gone to."

She shook the horrible thoughts of Philip from her mind, storing them away for later. "Just here, formatting my introduction for the story in my head, wondering how to keep these amazing abs out of it." Her hands trailed down the tight muscles that her body knew by heart, found their way to the deep V that led to his erection, now at full attention. She was only half kidding. It was increasingly hard to focus on her job when she was falling pretty fast for the boss.

"Oh, no, I think the world needs to hear about them. Please. It'll be the best PR I could ask for. Besides, I'm paying well for it, don't you think?" His smile sank to the crook of her neck where he sucked and nibbled at the skin until moisture that wasn't from the shower slid from between her legs.

From beneath her lust-induced coma, the fact that he'd said it would be the best PR he could ask for rose up from her subconscious. She'd been worried about him buying her approval. A chill coursed through her.

"And let all my journalistic integrity fly right out the window for eighty grand? I don't think so, Philip."

He didn't reply, but instead, bent down in front of her, using his hands to pull her legs more than shoulder-width apart.

She gasped as his kisses started at her stomach and

moved to the inside of her thighs. He trailed his tongue along the softest parts of her skin before reaching her center, which was wet and ready for him. Then he slipped a finger between her folds, and she braced herself against the marble walls of the shower, trying to find purchase. Another finger joined the first, pulling at her sensitive spot until a quiver of desire built inside her, threatening to spill over.

When his teeth grazed over her exposed nipples, she thought she almost came right there. But his mouth moved down her body again, until his tongue joined his fingers, trailing along her entrance, sucking as he pulled with his fingers in an exquisite dance of passion that moved her closer and closer to an orgasm she wasn't sure she could take standing up.

Journalistic integrity be damned. This was way more fun.

"More. Of you. I want you, Philip. Inside me." She gasped when he scooped her up on one arm and turned off the water with the other hand.

"You'd better be clean, my darling, because shower time is over."

He laid her down on the bed, her back sticking to the sheets. Philip looked down at her, his blue-green eyes stormy with emotion and desire. He was past the protective waters in the bay—they were treading in open water now. Her pulse quickened, knowing she was responsible for that.

"I want you," she told him, her voice thick with lust.

"You'll have me, all of me, in a moment. But first, I want you to have this." Philip reached over to the nightstand drawer and came back with another brown-paper-wrapped package for her, this one smaller than the rest.

Aurelia needed another bag to fit everything she'd accumulated on her week away from the castle, most of them gifts the Prince had given her on the trip. Every night, she'd come home from a walk on the beach to a single lily—her favorite—atop a brown paper-wrapped present on her bed. They'd started simple enough—the dress, then a matching pair of earrings the next night, but the night before he'd produced a stunning piece of art, a Kandinsky. And not a print, either. It was radiant, perfect, even, but too much.

The thing was, she had no idea how to tell Philip she couldn't accept the gifts. He'd offered to pay her to write a story about the royal family, so she was pretty sure he wasn't trying to buy her off, but then what? Why the extravagance when she was more than fine with just the trip?

"What is this?" she asked.

"Again, trying for the simple answers. Open it." He winked and bent to nibble on a bare breast, an evasive technique she didn't mind nearly as much. She tore at the paper and opened a silk-lined wooden box to reveal a necklace with her birthstone in the center, diamonds circling it.

She cried out, her hand covering her mouth. It was exquisite. And entirely too emotional a gift to receive from a man she'd just met. Somehow, he'd taken the little he knew of her and turned it into this spectacular piece of jewelry she couldn't keep.

The third night they'd spent at the beach house, she and Philip had finished off two bottles of wine and she'd started in about her mother, their shared connection with the water, how the cancer had taken her in less than six months and all but destroyed her and her dad. She'd described the pendant her father had bought her mother, a simple drop chain with a ruby in the center for her mother's birthday and how the hospital had lost it when her mother's body was transferred to the morgue. It had broken Aurelia's heart to lose the one physical reminder of her mother she wanted to take with her since anything else would be too big for Aurelia's apartment, too big to travel with her when she was on assignment.

That conversation and the first kiss they'd shared had led to a bonding between her and Philip she hadn't expected, and though her feelings for him grew in magnitude each moment they spent together, it wasn't to the point she could accept the necklace. Brian hadn't ever given her such a heartfelt gift and they'd been *married*. Not that he was the example to cling to, but still.

What did it say about her relationship with Philip that he would offer the jewelry?

What did she say in return by accepting it?

She reached behind her neck to secure the clasp, her hands shaking until his took over. Her growing feelings for Philip meant she couldn't turn down the thoughtful gesture, either. He looked down at her like she was the answer to all his problems, but the issue was, she had no idea what those problems were. He wouldn't open up to her about his life, his past, no matter how many times she said she wouldn't write about it. Something had happened to him that had obliterated his trust in women, and though she was pretty sure it was an ex, she still wasn't any closer to details that would help her make sense of the wall in front of her.

For starters, she hadn't gotten more than the basic history of the royal family from him to use in her interview. A few hundred years in liberated Aldonia, same royal bloodline the whole time, blah, blah, blah.

Everything she could find out with a simple Google search, basically.

Philip flat-out avoided any discussion of the King or his wife, except to say that he wished them every happiness. However, based on the growl that emanated from his chest when he said it, that was far from the truth.

He was a veritable stranger to her, but at the same time, he knew her well enough to knock her socks off—if she'd been wearing any socks—with his gift, the only thing she wore besides a smile as Philip unsheathed a condom and slid it on, the wooden box now back on the bedside table.

Another mystery for another day.

He slid his shaft inside her to the hilt, eliciting a cry from her as he drove deeper with each thrust. She put her hands on his athletic backside, pulling him closer to her. Maybe, hopefully, if she pulled him close enough, one of these times it would be what he needed to let loose. Because she had secrets of her own to share and she was beginning to think he was the one she wanted to share them with.

KRISTINE LYNN

CHAPTER EIGHT: ROYAL
QUESTIONS

Philip dug out his phone from the all-weather jacket he'd purchased in the city before making their way to the base of Mount Elbrus, the highest peak in Europe. He opened the camera app and snuck a photo of Aurelia as she ran down the rolling green foothills, laughing like a child at a playground, then slipped it back in its place before she noticed. He'd been doing the same thing all week, catching her as she walked from one room to the next, as she stepped outside to watch the waves roll in on one stormy night they'd had.

Against his better judgment, he'd taken one of her lying on her stomach while she slept, her hair wafting out above her in a brown and red waterfall, her tanned skin reflecting the moonlight as if she were made of the soft blue light. That was his favorite so far.

When Aurelia had crashed on the plane with exhaustion, he flipped through his photo reel to peruse the stolen moments he'd captured of her. Looking out over the water, her hands up at her chin, her teeth worrying her bottom lip. The waves behind her were rough that day, matching the mood he'd captured.

Another had Aurelia curled up in a chair on the patio with a book, her long, tan legs curled up underneath her, her finger in her mouth, brow furrowed in concentration.

He'd spent the entire hour flight recalling ways he'd fallen in love with this woman who'd come so unexpectedly into his life, upending it off its axis.

Love. That word had been swirling around in Philip's head since he and Aurelia shared a couple of bottles of expensive wine their third night at the beach house. She'd opened up and shared more about her mother, her passing, and that night, they'd made love like wild animals, desperate for each other's bodies in a way he'd never experienced before. Still, there was something she wasn't saying, and he was pretty sure it was about her previous relationship. He'd be hypocritical if he called her on it, though, so he stayed out of it. For now. The time was quickly approaching, though, when that wouldn't work for either of them.

"Come down here," she called up to him.

He smiled. Her energy, her passion—all of it was more addicting than the politics of governing a country, something he was born and bred to conquer. Now, it was only the supple, soft body of hers he couldn't get enough of.

He jogged down to her, the wind ruffling his hair, his legs remembering what it was like to let gravity take over. He was winded when he got to the bottom, but somehow, when Aurelia's lips met his, it was as if he hadn't walked a step.

"It's beautiful, isn't it?" she asked, spinning, her arms outstretched.

"It's nothing compared to you," he said.

He meant it, too. His country was scenic, majestic even, but seeing it through Aurelia's eyes gave him a sense of pride he'd somehow lost along the way.

"Ha ha, Casanova. Look at this. These mountains are

better than the Alps. Not that I've been to the Alps, but I feel like these are taller. Prettier. Do we really have to leave today?"

He was surprised. He'd thought she wanted to get back to the castle for her story. And he had a meeting with the royal treasury to discuss the upcoming fiscal budget.

"We do, but we can come back later next week. Although, I did want to take you to the winery when I'm done working Wednesday."

And a million other places if you'd just stay.

Forever.

"Are you sure? I can get Gregory to take me if you have things to do. I mean, there's no way you can take off an entire month just to entertain me."

"I can't, but I'll make it work. How about Wednesday?" The small lies like the one he just told her were starting to add up, weighing on him. He could take the year off if he wanted to, and God knew he didn't need to ever worry about money again in his, or his kids' lifetimes.

There was no way he was leaving the woman he was falling for alone with Gregory for any length of time, especially where alcohol was involved.

"Okay. Wednesday, then. That'll give me some time with your staff for another angle for the story." She kissed him perfunctorily on the lips and made her way back up the hill to the helicopter that would drop them both off at the jet to head home.

Home. He gave that word some thought—the idea of home and what it meant—as he walked. For the past week, he'd felt more at home in his modest beach house than he ever had in the palace, and a big reason, the biggest reason, actually, was Aurelia. Curling up with her on the couch while she read, waking to find her tangled in the comforter she'd stolen during the night, taking bits of food off her fork—each moment with her made him feel like any place he laid his head down at night would be home as long as she was there.

He didn't like the idea of being away from her until the middle of the week, but duty called. Hopefully, he'd be able to carve out time in the evenings with her, and while he worked, maybe he'd have the space he needed to sort out his feelings for her, decide how to tell her everything he'd been afraid to. Because one thing he was certain of was that Aurelia was not anything like *her*, and he didn't need to worry about her leaving him.

"I'd also like to talk to the locals," Aurelia added as she put on her noise-canceling headphones for the brief helicopter ride. "When I walked around town the night before our trip, they weren't exactly loving your brother's plan for medical coverage. I think it might be too constrictive—kinda like the country's education system. But we can get into that another time."

Philip adjusted his headphones. Had he heard her right? She thought Aldonia's policies were too constrictive?

"Are you comparing them to the U.S.?"

Aurelia laughed into her headpiece, shaking her head. "Um, no. We wrote the book on conservative approaches to both. I'm just looking at the rest of Eastern Europe and think it's time Aldonia got with the twenty-first century. People in the smaller towns have no access to affordable healthcare like those in the capital do, not to mention that many of them can't afford the premiums on the limited options for care plans. It's not altogether dissimilar to the U.S., actually. I hope this doesn't offend you. I know it's your country, but it's your brother's problem."

Philip tried a smile, but the futility of the gesture showed when it didn't reach his eyes.

"Yes, Robert's problem. And thank God for that, hmm?"

"I'd say. I wouldn't want any part of his life."

Philip's chest constricted. It was hard to breathe in a way that had nothing to do with the altitude they gained by the minute and everything to do with that throwaway comment from Aurelia.

She wanted nothing to do with Robert's life, but his wasn't much different. Suddenly, his future, the one he'd been working toward since the night his parents had died, was fractured in two. One of them sent him along the trajectory he'd been thrown on not of his own volition when he was fifteen. The other saw him relinquishing that future, and the responsibilities that came with it, for Aurelia. In none of the possibilities that flashed through his mind did he get to have both.

"Sorry," she added. "I'm just nervous in helicopters, and can't seem to shut off the part of my brain that vomits all my thoughts without prejudice." She giggled, her voice shaking as the helicopter dipped in altitude. Philip grasped her hand and kissed it.

How would he let it go, let *her* go in just under three weeks? His heart squeezed at the thought. It seemed more likely he'd give up the rest of it.

"You'll be okay. I'd never let anything happen to you."

She rested her head on his shoulder and went back to looking out the window while Philip considered what she said about Aldonia. She had a point about the changes that needed to be made to his country, and though he'd heard the criticisms before, he hadn't known what to do to fix the issue so he'd put it on the back burner for the time being. Maybe he'd talk to the budgetary council about some ideas that afternoon. He kissed the top of her head, thankful for her. Every day, she gave him a new reason to be so.

But how long would that last? How long could it?

When they arrived at the castle, Philip walked Aurelia back to her suite. He hadn't spent the night without her in a week. How was he supposed to sleep without her curvy, warm body pressed up against him? To do so here, though, would invite rumors, and he wasn't sure he was ready for that, either.

She stood on her toes, the necklace he gave her sitting

at the apex of her perfect breasts. Now that they were back amongst the rest of the castle staff and townspeople, his gift seemed mildly inappropriate. It called far too much attention to her exquisite cleavage. He'd have to make sure he gave her a sweater or something with a high collar to keep that view—the one he knew by touch and sight—to himself.

When her lips touched his, the now-familiar swelling in his jeans pressed against the fabric.

"Can I see you tonight?" she whispered against his neck, her breath hot on his skin.

"God, yes," he growled. The bulge in his pants grew, aching as he begrudgingly pulled himself away from her. He'd have to sneak back to his room, but it would be worth it.

Her hand dropped from his and he turned toward the Great Hall. As soon as he rounded the corner, he ran smack into Gregory, who leaned against the wall, one foot propped up underneath him, his arms crossed over his chest. It was the smug smile on his face that stopped Philip from just walking past. He didn't want to talk to his friend at that moment; he just wanted to shower off and get to work quickly so he could hurry back to Aurelia.

"What's that smile about?" Philip asked.

"I heard you were back a half hour ago, so imagine my surprise when I went to welcome you back, only to find you sucking face in the hallway. I'm guessing the trip went well?" Gregory laughed, but Philip wasn't in the mood.

Aurelia wasn't a joke to him.

"Piss off."

Gregory's laugh turned into a guffaw that echoed off the stone walls. "Oh, you are so screwed. C'mere. Let's talk."

Philip sighed, ran his hands through his hair. He could forgo his shower, but he'd better at least get out of his jeans first. The treasurer might have him committed if he showed up to the meeting this casual.

"Fine. But come to my place. I need to change."

"Yep. You got laid."

Philip's mouth screwed up in a retort that would have ruined his friendship if he gave a voice to it. Gregory's face softened, and he patted Philip on the shoulder.

"You really are screwed, aren't you?"

"You have no idea."

"And you won't say anything about shacking up, either? Must be serious."

"It is, buddy. It is." Philip sighed and Gregory's jaw visibly dropped.

"You aren't, you know, *falling for her*, are you?"

Philip nodded at the guards, who stood at attention on each side of the heavy oak, and dragged Gregory by the sleeve into his space when they'd opened his door.

"I think I am," he admitted when he was sure they were alone.

Gregory gave a loud laugh that sounded more like a bark, then whistled.

"She's incredible, smart, sexy as hell. Can you blame me?"

"Does she at least know about you and you-know-who?"

Philip shook his head again, this time, letting his chin drop to his chest.

"Jesus, man. How do you think that's going to go over when you tell her? Things are a little past that, don't you think?"

"Yeah, and that's not the only problem." Gregory gestured with his hands for Philip to continue. "She wants to talk about the 'constrictive medical coverage' and educational system we have in place. Seems she talked to the locals and they aren't happy."

"Well, crap, Philip."

Philip nodded, then paced the floor in his study, already wishing he was back in his jeans. He liked the relaxed lifestyle he'd had the past week and the constricting clothing he wore to represent his country felt like a straightjacket compared to the polo and pants he'd worn home.

"I don't have a freaking clue if I'm being honest. I just know it's another month and a half until the King gets back, and I need to talk to him. We need to hold her off."

"Ha!" Gregory spat out. "You'd have better luck taming a panther. What's your backup plan?"

Philip opened his mouth to reply that he really didn't have one when his phone buzzed on the table. He glanced down and saw his brother's number on the screen.

"Speak of the Devil," he muttered.

"Is that her already?"

Philip shook his head. "It's my brother."

Gregory's face lit up with an ear-to-ear smile. "Have fun with that and when you're off, text me a freaking plan."

"Will do." Philip swiped his phone to *answer* as Gregory slipped out silently. "Robert."

"Do you have a woman there? A woman you promised an exclusive story about our family?"

"Well, hello to you, too."

"Don't be coy with me, Philip. Do you?"

Philip sighed. Robert never pulled any punches, never settled for small talk. He was far too important for that.

"I do. Her name is Aurelia, and she's more than just 'a woman.'"

"But she's a journalist?"

"She is. She was invited by the royal family—I'm guessing your wife—and I asked her to stay. It's all pretty simple, Robert—I'm not sure what you don't understand."

Philip smiled, imagining the way his brother's cheeks and the tip of his nose turned red when he was angry, as he most certainly was now.

"Do you have any idea of the implications this could have for our family? How it could break the royal decree?"

"Yes, well, you can rewrite the decree, can't you? Isn't

that one of the perks of your position?"

"Are you really still jealous of me, Philip? Do you have any idea the kind of pressure I'm under?"

"This has nothing to do with you, Robert. I don't want anything to do with your position, and in fact, I've got a lot on my plate, too. I'm looking at changing the medical coverage laws we have, as well as the educational funding. Make them more accessible in rural areas."

There. He'd show his brother he was taking his role seriously. Finally. No need for Robert to know the journalist he was so worried about was the one who'd floated the idea.

There was silence on the other end for long enough that Philip coughed. "You still there?"

"I am," Robert replied. "Wow. I didn't realize you took our last talk seriously. If you need any advice, run it by me. I'm happy to share what I've learned in that department."

Philip smiled, this time without mirth. That was the kindest thing his brother had said to him in the past few years. Since his break-up with *her*. "I will, thanks."

"Let's talk about it more when I get home. Anyway, I'll let you talk to my wife. I suspect you're right about her issuing the invitation in the first place to deflect the coverage of her pregnancy. She's been rather grumpy about the whole thing lately."

Before Philip could say anything to get out of it, a deep, nasally sigh that he would recognize anywhere came through the line.

"Philip, darling."

He cringed. Her voice used to have the power to scare the piss out of him while at the same time eliciting a hard-on. It had been humiliating. Now, though? All he felt was pity infused with anger.

"Your Grace," he replied, his voice choppy and curt.

"You don't need to address me so formally. You don't do that with Robert."

"Robert didn't screw me over to get the title. I just

figured it's what you wanted, and you know I could never deny you any happiness."

It was true, but he spoke the words with a sarcasm he'd never had with her before. In fact, he realized this was the first time he'd spoken with Marjorie he didn't feel much of anything beyond annoyance.

Well, shoot. That was a development worth noting.

"You aren't being fair."

"Being fair wasn't part of the bargain. Now, is there anything you had in mind when you invited Aurelia here? I want to give her a story for her magazine, but I'm coming up short on acceptable topics that don't include you and me."

"Aurelia? The journalist? Just feed her your typical history of Aldonia bit. Anything to keep the story off my growing midsection. It's dreadful."

"I thought your growing midsection was a gift, but I understand. Problem is, we're past that. I've offered her an exclusive. I'm telling her about us."

"Why would you ever do such a thing? Isn't she already gone?"

"Nope. She's staying as my guest for the month."

There was another bout of silence, and Philip swallowed hard. He didn't want to get into this with her, not now. He had a meeting to get to, and then all he could think about was wrapping his arms around Aurelia again that evening. Preferably without clothing to hinder them.

"You like her, don't you?"

"I do. She's great. Smart, driven. Beautiful. Like you, but nicer."

He couldn't help the small jabs at Marjorie, feeling more than justified in dishing them out after the way they'd ended things.

"You know what I mean. Are you dating her?"

"You've lost the right to ask me questions like that. Enjoy your trip, Your Grace."

He hung up and realized his hands were shaking. In all

his time with Marjorie, or after they'd gone their separate ways, he'd never stood up to her, not sure what to say when a part of him still cared for her. Now, though, he'd been firm with both Robert and Marjorie in one phone call and felt better for it. Christ if Aurelia wasn't a good influence on him in more ways than one.

Philip jotted down some questions to ask at his meeting about the healthcare issue and a general markup of some ideas he had to run by the council. On the way to the Great Room, he stopped by the kitchen and asked for the executive royal chef, Patricia.

"Patricia, you genius. I need to ask a favor of you."

"Anything for you, Your Grace," the chef replied, kissing both Philip's cheeks as she looked behind him. "You're alone, then? How was your trip?"

"It was lovely, thank you. I need to ask if you can prepare a special dish for this Friday night?"

"Absolutely."

"It's not too late?"

"No, sir, and even if it were, we'd be delighted to take on a challenge. What did you have in mind?"

Philip wrote down the name he'd been given by Aurelia the night they'd drank their weight in wine. It was a dish her mother had made her each birthday, Aurelia's favorite dish in the world.

"This shouldn't be a problem at all. We have everything we need already in the storeroom. May I ask the occasion?"

"I just want to do something special for Aurelia."

Patricia winked and nodded. "Understood. Leave it to us, Your Grace. We'll see you tonight at seven?"

"Perfect, and thank you. This means a lot."

Philip had to admit that it felt good to hear her address him with his title. He'd been "Sir Philip" for so long now that he'd almost gotten used to that moniker, but in taking on the Budget Council and the medical care issues, he was finally getting back to his old self, the man he'd been destined to become.

Most of all, he wanted to be that man for Aurelia. He wanted to shed his secrets with her, and coax those she held close to her chest from her. He was done hiding from his life, living in the shadows.

He smiled and left the kitchens, knowing that he'd made progress toward the life he'd wanted for himself a long time ago. The words *Your Grace* echoed in his head, pushing his shoulders back the rest of the way to the meeting.

When the guards opened the door to the Great Room and the staff rose to meet him, he smiled.

"Good afternoon, everyone, and thanks for being on time. Now, settle in. We've got a lot to cover and not a lot of time to do it."

With that, Philip took the reins back and resumed his role as Philip, Duke of Puruse, Prince of Aldonia, second in line to become King. He let the corners of his mouth curl up into a proud grin.

Welcome back, Prince Philip. It was about darn time, too.

CHAPTER NINE: ROYAL PAINS

Aurelia's stomach roiled with nausea at the smell of the beef bourguignon the chef whipped up for her at Philip's request. Just a whiff of the flavorful stew was enough for bile to burn the back of her throat. Philip looked so happy about his special order with Patricia, the Irish head of staff and Royal Chef, that she had to at least attempt to stomach it, but she'd gagged and excused herself after trying to take a bite.

It was the fourth time Aurelia had thrown up in two days. It couldn't be the food because Philip had eaten all the same things as her each meal and he was healthy as a horse. Besides, between losing her lunch—and breakfast and everything in between—she felt fine. A little tired, maybe, but fine otherwise. Ugh. Why wouldn't it just pass, whatever was making her so sick? No one else seemed to be affected.

She hugged the rim of the marble sink, her ragged reflection staring back at her. Her curly hair stuck out from her ponytail like a lion's mane around the crown of her head. Her eyes were bloodshot, and her face white as a ghost despite the hours she'd spent reading in the gardens under the afternoon sun. She spit and washed her mouth out with the mint-flavored mouthwash each bathroom had on hand, feeling better with a fresh taste on her tongue. That didn't erase the fact that she somehow had to find a way to muscle through the rest of dinner with Philip, though. He'd been so thoughtful, recalling their conversation about her favorite dish. A dish her mother used to make her each birthday, one she'd never reacted to the way she was now.

Her arms braced against the sink as another wave of nausea rolled through her stomach and chest at the mere thought of food.

A knock at the door echoed in the large space, and the reverberation pounded in Aurelia's head. *Please don't let it be him.* If he caught her purging what little was left in her stomach, she'd be mortified. Especially since she'd kept the magnitude of her illness to herself until she could figure out what the problem was. Fortunately, at night, she felt infinitely better when his strong arms wound around her in the darkness, seeking her out, pleasuring her. But if she got him sick from those midnight intimacies, she'd never forgive herself.

"Coming," she whispered, barely able to push down the discomfort to cross the room. She ran her hands over her hair, smoothing what she could, and opened the door just enough to peek through. It was the head of the kitchens, Patricia, who she'd only barely started to get to know.

Patricia was an older woman of indiscernible age and a wicked sense of humor that came with a past as colorful as the woman's cheeks. She'd been with the royal family since her children were little, and now they all had children of their own. Aurelia had liked the chef from the moment she'd met her. Her presence, instead of making Aurelia uncomfortable, served to do the opposite. The vise grip on her head released ever so slightly.

"May I come in, dearie?" she asked Aurelia, who could barely muster a nod. "Good Lord, you look a fright."

Patricia shut the door behind her and put her hands on her ample hips. "Okay, love. Out with it. How far along are you, and does Philip know?"

Aurelia stared at Patricia through wide eyes, her jaw at her chest. She spun back around and dry heaved into the sink, beads of sweat forming on her brow.

"I can't be," she whispered when the convulsions abated.

"Aye, but that doesn't change the fact that you are, dear. Now come, sit down."

Patricia led Aurelia to the edge of the bathtub where she all but shoved Aurelia down onto her backside as she fussed over her. Patricia gave her a cool washcloth and instructed her to put it on her forehead, which almost immediately calmed the pounding in her head.

Tears sprang to Aurelia's eyes.

"Now, now. It isn't anything to be upset about. Women've been dealing with this little surprise since the beginning of time and all of 'em have found their way around the news. You weren't trying for this, I gather?"

Aurelia shook her head.

"That's what I expected. But Philip's a good man, and he'll do right by ya—whatever it is you decide to do. Now, I'm gonna go scrounge up some crackers and tea. You stay right here, and I'll tell Philip to wrap up your dinner 'til you're feeling better."

Aurelia nodded, then froze.

"Patricia?"

The woman turned around, a gentle smile softening her features.

"You won't tell him, will you?"

Patricia shook her head. "That's not my secret to share. You take your time, dearie. But don't wait too long. He's bound to notice you're under the weather sooner or later."

Aurelia nodded again, still otherwise frozen with the magnitude of the news she'd feared but managed to talk herself out of. They'd been using protection for two weeks, and the last person she'd slept with before that was her ex-husband a year and a half earlier. She wasn't completely clueless—of course, she was aware it could happen whether or not protection was used—but that didn't make her any more prepared for the fact that it *had* happened.

No, no, no, no, no, her brain repeated. *Not possible. Not okay.*

What would she do? She was on assignment, which meant she'd created a major conflict of interest when she started sleeping with a member of the royal staff—the member who was paying her no less—so what would happen now that she was pregnant with his baby?

Pregnant. With Philip's baby. The Prince's baby.

That made the baby growing inside her a… a prince as well?

She spun back around and vomited into the sink again, this time less because of the nausea and more out of fear for the predicament she found herself in.

Pregnant with the Prince's child.

The words tumbled around in the back of Aurelia's mind and throat, making her dizzy again. She turned on the cold water and refreshed the damp towel for her forehead that was scalding hot already.

This was most definitely a problem, especially because Philip still wouldn't talk to her about his past. So how was she supposed to irrevocably alter his future? He'd never mentioned what would happen between them when she left the castle once her assignment was over, nor had he said anything about kids—wanting them or otherwise. Though now that she thought about it, he got awkward every time Aurelia mentioned the Queen and the fact that she was expecting.

Damn it. Times a thousand.

A knock on the door jarred her from the war she waged with her thoughts and feelings.

"Come in," she called, expecting Patricia with

reinforcements that she might be able to stomach.

Instead, in some cosmic twist of cruel fate, Philip walked in, a vision in jeans and a jet-black button-down shirt rolled up to show off his strong forearms that strained against the fabric. More than once, those arms had been wrapped around her, or had held her up against the wall as they made love. Knowing what they were capable of made it hard to look at them—a problem now exacerbated by the fact that those forearms were more than a little responsible for the precarious position she found herself in.

"Babe," he said, putting a hand between her shoulder blades and rubbing gently. "What's going on? Did you catch something? I told you we shouldn't have swam so late at night. Especially in that disgusting lake. This is my fault—I should have stayed firm and not let you jump in."

A sob escaped Aurelia's throat, unburdening her from having to hold it in any longer as she shook her head no, trying to absolve him. Sure, they shouldn't have gone skinny dipping in the small lake. But all the armed forces in all the world couldn't have kept her from catching what really ailed her. She'd made love to him in the lake, in his bed, on top of the down comforter that had made her feel like she was a thousand feet above the Earth on a cloud, and a dozen other places she couldn't recall.

She retched again, nothing coming up this time because she was empty. She had nothing left. All those times she'd been unable to say no to herself were why she was so sick now—and would be for the next nine months.

She cried harder, her whole body shaking. She would hate him seeing her like this if she had a spare ounce of energy to devote to anything other than not succumbing to the fear, the wish to disappear on the spot.

"There, there. Let's get you into bed, love." At this, a feral cry came from deep within Aurelia's chest. Those words, both what he said and how he said them, broke her in half. He'd uttered the same incantations each time he'd undressed her, touched her body with his strong but gentle hands in a much more sensual way than he did at that moment. And those words, said now with such care and love, would disappear altogether once he found out what was really wrong with her.

A sickening list of questions pelted the back of her mind, bringing back the pulsing ache.

Would he think she planned this to trick him into marriage? Would she be bound to him forever now that she carried an heir to the throne? She wasn't meant for this life any more now than when she first arrived and the thought of being forced into it turned the pounding in her head into a thunderous storm.

Philip whisked Aurelia up in his arms. Though the abrupt movement was jarring, her pulse slowed and her chills abated the second her head pressed against his chest. She inhaled his scent and remarkably, the nausea dissipated as well. The stark relief was so pleasant, so needed.

Aurelia was only mildly aware of being taken into Philip's suite, of being laid down with expert care underneath the cloud-like comforter. Her eyes shut, exhaustion taking over the energy that was previously reserved for keeping her upright, getting food into her system. Now, none of that seemed as important as resting, as letting her eyes shut against the reality she wasn't ready to face.

When Aurelia's eyes fluttered open, daylight peeked through the top of the drawn curtains. She rubbed her eyes and took in her surroundings. The light was bright and nestled high above her, meaning it must be sometime around noon. That meant she'd slept over twelve hours. God, she must have needed it. Everything else was unfamiliar. How hadn't she seen his bedroom yet? It was one more part of his life he kept closed off from her. One more inaccessible facet in his stoic professionalism with her outside of her bedroom.

The bed was larger than hers, but just as comfortable.

The oak dresser bore different carvings than those she'd curled up next to the past two weeks.

The unique scent of cinnamon and pine tickled her nose rather than the salt and vanilla that permeated her room.

She was in Philip's suite, but couldn't appreciate the grandeur that made her palatial guest suite look like a motel room in the Bronx.

Her chest filled with the now-familiar pang of nausea, of bile building with no place to go but out. She braced herself against the first wave, then noticed a plate of crackers and a mug of steaming tea by her bedside—or Philip's bedside, rather.

She may have been in his room, but he wasn't anywhere to be found. To that end, the bed next to her was made up on the other side, leaving the question of whether he'd been there at all. She snatched a cracker and devoured it, barely chewing she was so hungry.

"Slowly," Patricia said, coming out of the sitting room attached to Philip's bedroom with laundry folded in a basket. "You won't keep them down if you act like a momma bear coming out of hibernation."

"I feel like a momma bear," Aurelia said, taking Patricia's advice and nibbling slower this time. "I'd eat an animal carcass, I'm so hungry." Though as soon as she'd uttered the words, her body revolted against the idea and her throat gagged on bile.

Patricia chuckled.

"Some tea, too, dearie. It'll help calm the nausea. And nothing else until your stomach settles."

Aurelia nodded, sipped at the tea between bites, and noticed how much the symptoms calmed with just a few bites.

"Ugh. Thank you. I haven't felt this good in days. Will I be able to eat anything else other than these crackers?"

Patricia nodded, putting clothes in the endless drawers, hanging others in the massive walk-in closet the room boasted.

"In time. But every morning, I want you to eat the plate of crackers and finish the cuppa before you put your feet down on the ground. It'll make getting through the day easier if you take care of your cravings before anything else. For lunch, I'll have you brought some toast and jam. The sugar'll be good for you and the lil' miss you're growing."

Aurelia winced. She'd temporarily forgotten the reason why she felt so crappy. It was the worst possible situation. As much as she appreciated the help from Patricia, at that moment, Aurelia wanted her mother. She wanted to be held as if she were a child herself, without judgment or concern.

Tears sprang to her eyes, imagining having to tell her father about this…situation.

"There, there. You'll be okay. I've asked to be the one to care for you so I can make ya what you need. I birthed and raised five babies, lost two more beyond that, so I reckon I've got a thing or two to say on the matter."

"You haven't told Philip?" Aurelia asked, taking a bigger bite of cracker this time. She didn't make eye contact with Patricia, afraid of what the woman's face might reveal. She'd been nothing but patient with Aurelia, but that didn't mean she didn't have feelings on the subject.

"Like I said, it's not my news to share. Though if you want my advice, I'd get that part over with sooner rather than later. He's worried about you and that's not liable to change any time soon. Plus, not to worry ya, but there's the issue of lineage you'll have to discuss. Your lil' miss is a royal, and that comes with certain privileges, but also responsibilities."

Aurelia nodded. Telling Philip was easier said than done. How the heck would she broach something as sensitive as a baby with a man she'd only been seeing a couple of weeks? She didn't even know how she felt about the whole thing, honestly. Other than nauseated.

She'd also like to find out more about him first—how he felt about kids, heck, how he felt about *her*, but any conversation she started along those lines was bound to make him suspicious.

"I'll tell him soon. I just have to figure out how."

"I've often found that the honest truth is the best way. If you're straightforward with him, he'll be fair with you. I'm not guaranteeing he'll be over the moon—it takes men a lot longer to work their way around their feelings about becoming a parent—but if he treats you poorly, you let me know and I'll wallop him."

Aurelia laughed, though the whole situation was decidedly not funny.

"Where is he?" she asked Patricia.

"Gone for the day. He'll be back for dinner, though. Made sure to tell me he wanted time alone with you before he left, so you'll have your chance to talk to him without any distractions."

No distractions. Except for the tiny human that was growing by the minute in Aurelia's body. She put her hand to her stomach, hoping to feel different somehow, but all she felt was sick, tired.

"Did he say why he brought me here, to his suite?"

"He didn't, and I didn't ask. If I had to guess, he wanted to keep you close, to care for you in the way he can. He might not always do the right thing at the right time, but he comes to it eventually."

It was sweet, but like Patricia said, it didn't mean he wouldn't be appalled, pissed even, at the news. It was all fun and games sleeping with the American until the birth control didn't work and they had to cope with what that meant for them both. And to think she'd imagined her nausea to be the result of too much wine when they visited the royal winery. Ha.

Crap. The winery. She'd been pregnant then.

"Patricia," Aurelia called, her voice laced with panic.

"*Patricia!*"

The woman came shuffling, as close to a run as she could muster, breathless and petrified.

"What's the matter, dearie? Do you need to use the facilities? I'll have a chamber pot brought to your bedside so you don't have to get up."

Aurelia shook her head. "No, sorry. I'm fine. At least I think I am. But I drank so much wine last weekend. Is the baby going to be…"

She couldn't finish the sentence. A fierce wave of protection rolled over her. Her heart raced and her veins raged with heat at the idea she might have done something to jeopardize the small life they'd created. It may not have come at the opportune time, but her heart surged with love for the tiny human.

"Oh, love. The baby will be just fine. I had a good bit of brandy each night for the first two months of each pregnancy before I knew. How Reginald loved his fancy nightcaps. Anyway, don't have any more and you'll be just fine. All the more reason to tell Philip, though. He'll begin to wonder why you don't join him for wine with your meals anymore."

The woman patted Aurelia on the head and pulled the now-empty laundry basket to her hip.

When Patricia left the room, Aurelia gingerly made her way to the shower. She needed to process everything. The heat sank into her pores, to muscles that ached from being bent over porcelain all day the past few days.

She thought about what to tell Philip, ruling out grabbing her passport and running for the border, leaving a note to explain their issue. The whole thing was complicated by the fact that she hadn't written a freaking word of her story. If she left now, she'd be forfeiting the last couple of weeks of work, not to mention money enough to erase her debt, plus save for all the baby would need. Diapers, food, clothes… The list went on. If she didn't write and she didn't get what she came for, she wouldn't get paid.

It was crap, all of it.

Philip had been so sweet to her, taking her all over the country to show her the sights, the history of the land and its owners, but when it came to why she was there, she hadn't accomplished anything of value except a scathing introduction about the pedantic ways of the foreign country that, of course, she'd never use.

All of that was before she'd slept with Philip, fallen for him.

When they'd gotten back from the Black Sea, she'd made three separate appointments with Gregory, hoping to interview him on the growing list of questions her travels with Philip produced about their friendship, Philip's childhood. All three appointments were rescheduled for "urgent business," which was bull, considering he was either saying goodbye rather seductively to one of his female overnight guests, or joking with the staff.

Nothing looked too urgent to her, but then again, she didn't know what he did each day because the man refused to speak with her. That, and Philip was hiding something personal from her. Sure, she harbored her own secret—well, two secrets now—but until Philip came clean, she just couldn't say anything about her situation.

Thinking about Gregory, about Philip and his secrets, gave her an idea. She smiled for the first time in days, feeling her old self resurface. Maybe there was a way she could kill two birds with the same shot.

Aurelia toweled off quickly and made sure to do her makeup in the professional way she usually wore it when she was on assignment. Once she'd shown up to the Black Sea with Philip, had kissed him on the beach, all pretenses had been discarded and she'd settled for a simple application of mascara and nothing more. Now, though, she would play the part she'd arrived to accomplish. She secured her hair in a tight bun, ignoring the fact that pulling on her temples made her headache from the day before resurface.

Picking up her phone, she texted the number she knew by heart at this point.

I need to talk to you. Urgent. Meet me at my suite.

With a smug, tight smile, Aurelia pulled up the comforter on Philip's bed, snatched up her small bag that lay beside it, and made her way back to her room, the plan solidifying along the way.

Not ten minutes later—just enough time to set up a workstation and get her questions and notes organized—there was a knock on her door. She rose to get it and bit back a wave of dizziness that threatened to derail everything. She took a sip of the tea she'd brought along with her and opened the door to a worried-looking Gregory.

"You're right on time, sir. Come in." She ushered him to her table and offered him a glass of water—all she could stomach outside of tea.

"What is it? You said it was urgent. Is it Philip? Where's he gone? Jesus, is he hurt?"

"Philip is fine. Have a seat."

"Aurelia, you're scaring me. What is so urgent you needed me here so quickly?"

"It's the only way I could get you to meet with me, and honestly, I should have thought of it sooner."

"Wait, this was all to get me here for your interview? Not cool, Aurelia. I ran all the way here thinking something was the matter." Gregory stood, running his hands through his hair. "Inventive—I'll give you that, but not cool," he added.

She smiled, her lips thin and drawn.

"I pulled the page from your book, so you should be proud."

"What do you mean?"

"You keep blowing me off telling me you have urgent business to attend to, but all I've been able to piece together is that 'urgent business' is code for 'hooking up with someone.'"

Gregory smiled, his straight white teeth glowing in the light. She had to admit, his charms weren't lost on her—he was handsome as the Devil and had a way with women, but her heart was taken by his best friend. In another world, she'd have loved to have a relationship with someone like Gregory—uncomplicated, fun, and downright sexy—but there was no changing her feelings for Philip.

"You disagree about the urgency of a beautiful woman in my bed?"

God, how this man helped run a successful country, she had no idea. He was more court jester than he was royal advisor.

He winked, and she thought of Philip, the way he winked down at her when he was on top of her, his strong arms propping her up. Her stomach flipped with desire at the same time her head pounded its disapproval of the feeling. Everything about this place, these people, reminded her of the man she'd come to love, to need.

"Fine. I get it. But in case you've forgotten, Philip is paying me $80,000 to write about something he won't tell me. Since you know him best, you either come clean, tell me what I'm staying here to hear, or I'm leaving."

He narrowed his gaze, attempting a look that matched hers in its intensity, but the corners of his lips twitched in a subdued smile he couldn't hide.

"You're good at this game," he finally said, crossing his arms over his well-defined chest.

"I darn well should be. I've been doing it long enough."

"Okay, well, you might not want to hear this, but I don't have a story for you." He tossed her an award-winning smile along with a shrug that seemed to imply an apology of some sort.

A very weak apology as far as she was concerned.

"You're kidding me, right?"

He'd better be…

"I'm not. I mean, I have some things I could tell you that would definitely be newsworthy," he said, adding a whistle and laugh, "but they aren't my stories to tell."

Aurelia sucked air in through clenched teeth, hoping to come off at least semi-professional. She'd been there before, promised a story only to have the informant or witness back out at the last minute, afraid of the consequences. But she'd never—*never*—been told to screw off with a flip of a hand and a laugh.

Like this was all some kind of joke.

"I don't care whose story it is. Philip is avoiding talking about it, which is killing my story and any hope of a relationship we might build. You get how ridiculous this all is, right? Him with his stoicism and secrecy, while you parade around like a prince and cover for him. Why don't both of you start acting like men and help me do the job he hired me to do?"

She closed her eyes and exhaled slowly, a crushing vise grip clenching her head. With it bubbled up nausea that seemed a now-permanent part of her genetic makeup, waiting until the least-opportune moments to rear its ugly head. She lifted her head, her lips a tight line that she hoped showed her utter lack of patience with Gregory, with Philip, with the whole cursed palace.

"Aurelia, I like you, I do. But I can't tell you whose story it is. Not without talking to them first. I'm sorry, and I feel bad, but my hands are tied."

He was uncharacteristically serious. That unnerved Aurelia more than his typical joking.

"So, you can't tell me the story because it's someone else's to tell, and you can't tell me whose it is, because that's not something they'd like you to share, either? Do you hear how absolutely asinine you sound? Sorry. Do you hear how absolutely asinine you sound, *sir*?"

She spat out the last word like a curse, her pulse racing.

While she waited for Gregory to answer her, her chest

constricted. She only had about three seconds until she lost the crackers and tea she'd had recently. She got up and ran for the trash can, only to find it wasn't in the place by her bed where she'd left it the day before.

No, no, no.

Before she could figure out her next move, she heaved and everything she'd eaten that morning came up, most of it landing on her shirt. She shook, tears streaming down her face, when a hand pressed on the small of her back.

"I'm sorry. I didn't mean to make you so upset," Gregory said, his voice gentle, serious.

Aurelia shook her head. "Not you. Just… sick," she managed to get out.

"What can I do?" he asked, rubbing her shoulders. "Want me to see if anyone is around who can bring you medicine? I think the chef might be able to help if I ask."

"A shirt. Clean. The drawer." She pointed to an ornate chest of drawers she'd unpacked her things into when she'd been offered the month-long stay and exclusive story. Ha. What a joke it all was now, a joke she'd fallen for hook, line, and sinker. Philip wasn't ever going to give her anything. He paid her for a puffed-up PR piece and had paid her enough in cash and sex to expect what he bought.

"Aurelia," Gregory's voice came from the other side of the room, "there isn't anything here, in any of these."

She wiped her mouth with the sleeve of her shirt and stood up, feeling weak but better, less nauseated.

"What do you mean?"

But he was right. There wasn't a shred of clothing in any of her drawers. The tears came stronger now and a feeling of defeat washed over her, drowning her sorrows. She'd come to Aldonia at the invitation of the royal family, but had been asked by Philip to cover something more important, something only he could offer.

Now she had nothing. No story, no interview— nothing but a baby inside her that she wasn't sure the father would even want.

The father, Philip.

Philip.

Of course it was his story, but when he wasn't making Aurelia swoon with desire, he was as tight-lipped as a priest. In not sharing it with her, he not only made her job null, he axed their relationship as well. She'd done the moody, secretive guy before and had no desire to repeat the mistake.

She shuddered as a sob wracked her chest.

He'd also probably taken all her clothes and belongings to his suite. Crap. Her toothbrush was nowhere to be found, either.

It was so damned controlling, thinking he could just move her in with him without even asking her permission, asking what she'd like to do. It was something Brian would have done. *Had done*, she corrected herself.

"Here," Gregory said, pulling his shirt over his head. She averted her eyes, because even though she wasn't attracted to him, she had to admit he was beautiful. The fact that he was still single was purely due to his choice.

"I can't," she said, sniffling. But one glance at the clean, dry t-shirt he offered, her instincts took over and she snatched it out of his hands. "Fine. Thank you," she said, more curt than she meant her voice to sound. He was being nice when he didn't have to, when he could kick her out of the country and no one would ever have to deal with her in Aldonia again.

She wasn't sure if that would be a blessing or a curse.

"You're welcome. Here, let me help you."

As much as she wanted to refuse his help, she couldn't change on her own. It was as if she'd run a marathon and contracted the flu all in the same day. He pulled her soiled blouse over her head and shimmied her out of her jeans. She didn't care at all that she was standing there in her bra and panties—and not the cute kind, either, since she'd felt too crappy to attempt to look attractive when she'd dressed the night before.

"I'm not contagious," she whispered.

"Whew. That's a relief," he said, laughing. "You know I don't care, Aurelia. You're like a sister to me, and I'd take care of you even if you had the plague."

She choked out a laugh that doubled as a sob, more tears falling as he embraced her and held her tight against him. His arms were the only thing keeping her upright.

Just as she was about to ask for the shirt so she could crawl into her bed and sleep the rest of the day away as well, get a clear head, a growl of pain came from the other side of the room by the door.

Gregory pulled back and muttered an expletive, threw his hands up in the air like he'd been caught mid-burglary by the cops.

"Philip," he said, his voice thick and grave.

Philip. Aurelia's heart filled at the sound of his name. He was there, hours before she expected him, and when she needed him most.

"Hey, babe," she said, her voice sounding distant and dreamy to her ears. She waved, which was stupid, but she only had seconds before her body mutinied and she fell to the bed. Her vision wavered in and out. How anyone worked through pregnancy feeling this awful was beyond her. *Please let this pass. Let the baby be okay.*

"What's going on here?"

Gregory walked over to Philip, but Philip threw a hand up, stopping him in his tracks. Why was he staring at Gregory's bare chest?

Oh, yeah. Gregory wasn't wearing a shirt. She was wearing it because she'd thrown up on hers. Except she wasn't wearing anything either. In slow motion, like a freeze-frame of horror on the big screen, Aurelia realized with sickening reality what was happening. What Philip must be thinking.

"Philip, it's not what it looks like," she said, her voice shaking as he backed up in disgust. "I threw up," she started, but he was out the door, Gregory on his heels hollering for his friend to wait, to let them explain.

With that, Aurelia was alone in her room, her sobs echoing off the tall stone walls. When she calmed down, realizing no one was coming for her to check in on her health, to tell her they understood, she collapsed on the bed.

"I think we're doing this alone," she told the life inside her. No mother, no friends, no husband. Just her, as usual. That was the last thing she thought before she faded off into blackness, her only chance at escaping the nightmare her life had become.

CHAPTER TEN: ROYAL MISUNDERSTANDING

Philip sprinted down the corridor without a clue where he was headed.

Flashes of Marjorie came to the back of his lids like a highlight reel of his worst moment. Until this one. This was decidedly worse because he and Marjorie hadn't been in love. But he, without a shadow of a doubt, had fallen for Aurelia. He'd even asked her to keep some time that night for just them so he could tell her, to ask her to stay indefinitely.

Jesus. Oh, God, why did this always happen to me?

As if his best friend—well, *former* best friend—could read his mind, Gregory caught up to him, put his hand on Philip's shoulder, and squeezed.

"She's not Marjorie. She'd never do that to you," he said, breathless yet still bare-chested. Anger flooded Philip's veins, careening through him wild and rapid.

"Well, it looks like she did, doesn't it?" Philip shoved Gregory's hand off. He needed to punch something, was afraid it would be Gregory if the man didn't back off.

Couldn't he read between the freaking lines?

"She didn't, though. Would you just listen to me?" he yelled.

Philip paced the hallway between his room and Aurelia's. Crap. He'd just had Patricia move Aurelia into his suite. That would be awkward now, wouldn't it? At least Marjorie had moved to the other castle so Philip hadn't needed to see her, work with her every day. Would Aurelia want to move in with Gregory now? Philip's chest heaved just imagining it, though little was left to his imagination after seeing the two people he loved most in the world nearly naked and pressed up against each other. He shuddered, heat building behind his eyes.

Again. It had happened again.

"At least you had the good sense not to sleep with her on my bed. I would have killed you for that."

"Fine. If you aren't going to listen to me, that's your deal. But you'll lose everything you've been looking for if you're stubborn about this, Philip. I've seen how you two look at each other, and that doesn't come around every day. Believe me—I've slept with half the damn country and I'm no closer to finding what you had fall in your lap. What you're about to give up for pride. Wake up, Philip—it doesn't get better than her."

Gregory left him there, standing in the dark hallway, wishing he would have just waited until dinner to see Aurelia. What he wouldn't have known wouldn't have tried to kill him like seeing her with his best friend had done. He balled up his fist and hit the wall with as much force as he could muster.

He roared, blinding pain shooting up his arm, his fist collapsed at his side, his fingers limp. He'd done enough stupid crap in his life to know his fingers were broken—maybe the metacarpals, too—which just pissed him off even more. He should get checked out with the medical team, but before he did, he needed to know Aurelia's side of things.

How long had she been interested in Gregory? Was it

his way with women or Philip's lack of it? Would everything be different if he'd just been honest with her about Marjorie? But then she would have just gotten better at hiding it, wouldn't she?

Without knowing how he'd arrived there, he found himself outside Aurelia's door. Knocking was out since a glance down at his right hand showed it swollen and already turning a color purple that he'd only seen when he'd boxed—and even then, only on his opponents.

He walked into the room that was darker than the hallway. The blinds were shut, but he made out a soft snore followed by a whimper. How could she fall asleep within seconds after he caught her cheating on him? His teeth chattered, sounding like a hammer drill in the otherwise silent space.

He strode over to where she lay and watched her chest rise and fall, her lips parted and at peace. Oh, well, screw it. If he didn't get to be at peace, neither did she. He shook her shoulder, hoping to rouse her.

All he managed, though, was to rile a bigger snore from her, then she rolled over, her back to him. He tried again, but nothing. She didn't move a muscle. What the—?

"Philip Anthony, you leave that girl alone. She is sick as a hound, and I'll not have you making it worse."

Philip glared up at Patricia, his favorite member of staff, his eyes narrowed. He'd always wished she and Petre, his father's Head of Guard, would get together when their spouses had both passed on before their time, but at that moment, he didn't give a damn what she thought. He needed to talk to Aurelia, and it had to happen *now*.

"Patricia, I love you, but you need to butt out. This is none of your concern."

"The Devil it isn't, young man. And none of this 'I love you, but' nonsense. I love you, but if you touch that girl again, you'll have to answer to me."

"You don't know what she did. I have to talk to her." His voice cracked. He hated that he was caught in a moment of weakness, his crushed heart on his sleeve for the whole freaking castle to see.

"I know she loves you, Philip, that the secret she's holding inside her needs to be shared, but I also know she needs her sleep. Go for a run and cool off. I've got to get this girl dressed. Seems she lost her lunch on her nice new shirt, and you took everything the poor lass owns into your room."

Philip left Aurelia alone, but he couldn't stand just yet. She had thrown up? That was why she was all but naked with his best friend? Nothing had happened between them?

She'd thrown up, and Gregory had offered his shirt to keep her comfortable. It seemed a reasonable enough excuse. Plausible, even. Heck, the door was wide open, after all. It wasn't like they'd been trying to hide anything. The hint of a smile tugged at Philip's lips.

But it didn't last long.

He just couldn't erase the image of Gregory holding Aurelia in his arms, couldn't get past the way it opened up his chest, carved out his heart when he pictured it. There was no explaining that one away, at least not without hearing Aurelia's side of the story, or giving Gregory the benefit of the doubt.

He wasn't calm enough for either of those options, yet.

"I'll be in my office. See that she finds me before dinner."

He strode toward the door, pausing only when he heard Patricia call out softly, "She'll find you when she's good and ready, young man, and not a minute sooner."

He sighed and left. He was on his own, then. He'd pushed everyone away, and he couldn't escape the thought that despite what he'd witnessed, what he'd worried had occurred, he was the one who'd screwed up.

Again.

The same plaguing fear had all but crippled him when he'd caught Marjorie in bed with his brother. What if he'd been more open to love, been less regal, more human? What if he could have shed the thick walls that hid him away from the outside world, walls he'd built after his parents had died? That day had cemented the walls, barring him from letting anyone in, or any of himself out.

Of course, only far too late had he realized that Marjorie had her own challenges in their relationship that had nothing to do with Philip, but maybe it would have been easier to see them if he'd just broken down some of the barrier. Instead, she'd cheated—and with his brother no less—adding to the height and depth of the wall that barricaded his heart.

It was as if Aurelia was a sledgehammer, shattering the bricks and mortar, shining light in places that hadn't seen out of the shadows in far too long. The past two weeks he'd felt relieved as fresh air rolled over him, but at the same time, he was certain that if the same woman responsible for giving him that freedom betrayed him, the walls would go back up forever. Impenetrable and all-encompassing.

The day had faded into dusk, and even that was on its way out when Philip heard a knock on his office door. It was so quiet the first time, he couldn't be sure it wasn't just the creaking of aging wood, but a few seconds later, it came louder, clearer.

"It's open," he said. He steadied his trembling hands by gripping the desk, hoping the tremor would go unnoticed. There wasn't a time he could recall being that nervous, but then, he'd never had as much to lose, either.

Aurelia opened the door and peeked inside. Her hair was damp, but there was more color to her cheeks than there'd been earlier. Still, though, something was off with her, different.

"You wanted to see me?" Her voice was soft, as if the breeze from outside had carried it from a great distance.

With that one question, he almost went to her, told her everything. That he loved her, that even if she had slept with Gregory, he wanted to be with her.

That despite the hell Marjorie had put him through, he was capable of love again.

Something stopped him, though, like an invisible hand pressed against his chest that wouldn't let him move an inch.

"I did." The words came out gruff, but damn it all, he was on the verge of tears and couldn't give her the upper hand—not yet.

She came all the way in the room and for the first time, he noticed how small she was, how frail she'd become. His hands gripped the desk tighter, so that his knuckles turned pale. His fingers ached to release the cold metal and run a hand down her gaunt cheek. What about living there with him was making her so ill?

"Nothing happened, Philip."

All he could do was nod. Of course, it hadn't. So then, why couldn't he make his way to her? Hold her like Gregory had, comfort the woman he loved like she clearly needed to be comforted? It was so easy for Gregory, but it never had been for him. Why not?

Because there is a country on the line, a voice chimed in from his subconscious. *You have a duty to serve others besides yourself.* The last time he'd been betrayed, he'd nearly taken his country down with him. If it weren't for Gregory stepping up to fill his shoes, there would have been a major problem facing Aldonia.

Philip had failed them.

"Do you want to hear this? Because I'm at the end of my rope. I came here thinking I was invited by the royal family, that they wanted me to write about the Prince, about *you,* but then you asked me to stay. You offered me more than anyone has ever given me, and not just professionally, either. I've been killing myself to get the story, to get *you,* but you were never going to give any of it to me, were you?"

Well, Christ.

Philip was genuinely struck dumb for a moment, or at least mute. He opened his mouth to contradict what she'd accused him of, only to realize that she was right, at least on some level. It wasn't in his plans at all to give her the story he'd promised her because that would mean he'd have to give more of himself to her than he had ever given anyone before, and frankly, that scared the hell out of him.

But that didn't mean he was ready to lose her, either.

He took a step toward her but she mirrored it, moving away from him, her hand raised in defiance. Her fingers were sallow, thin, like her cheeks.

"Aurelia," he begged, his voice dripping with desperation, "Please. Let me just explain and you'll see. I didn't mean to hurt you. I just wanted you around for some reason I hadn't figured out yet. Promising a story was the only thing I could think of to make that happen."

"And now? Do you want me around now?"

"Of course, I do. Jesus. I'm in love with you."

Her mouth opened as if she wanted to reply, her eyes bright and wide, but then just as quickly, a shadow passed over her face, and her mouth closed again.

"Then give me something. Anything that makes me feel like you want me, need me as much as I need you. Tell me *your* story, and not because I'll publish it, but because you don't want me to leave. Because, make no mistake, Philip. If you don't, right here and now, I am gone. Forever. Too much is at stake to do this halfway."

Oh, God. Could he do it? Could he give her everything she was asking for, in order to get everything he'd ever wanted? His heart beat out an enthusiastic *Yes!* But his head cautioned him, flashed another image of Marjorie and his brother in bed together.

"I—I don't know."

"Have you checked your email, Philip? Do it now, while I'm here. I want you to see how I saw this country when I first got here, how I saw you." She crossed her arms, waited while he opened up his email and read line by line the most honest, scathing portrayal of him, of his country.

"This is your story?" he asked. She'd seen him as he truly was, even if she didn't know it was him she wrote about at first. His hands shook with rage, with fear. He was already exposed, he just hadn't realized how transparent he was all along.

"It was going to be, until I met you and saw the changes you've been trying to make. Until I fell in love with you. I'll never print that story now, but you have to know it's how the world sees you. What are you going to do to fix this? Do you even want me around while you do it?"

God, he did. Hell, she was responsible for all the good he'd accomplished in the past month. But the fear gripped tighter, clamped down on his tongue so he couldn't say a word, let alone what Aurelia needed to hear.

"Fine. Then, goodbye. Thank you for the most wonderful three weeks. I'll never forget them, or you, Philip."

She walked out the door, and Philip waited.

She'd come back, right? She'd walk back in and see that he was just being a coward, that he loved her, that if she could just be patient, eventually, he'd open up to her. He was trying, making small strides.

Wasn't that enough?

So, he waited. For three hours, he sat there, going through other emails, writing briefs for his councils on the economics of Aldonia, the ways he could improve an already solid budget. In between, he got his injured hand wrapped and seen to. Yes, it was broken, but cleanly. It would heal. Unlike the rest of him. The minutes ticked by, the mountain of paperwork in front of him growing.

He really did see the potential to make into law a mandatory minimum health insurance coverage policy that dictated a standard required to be issued free of cost for each citizen of the country, additional choices available after that. In fact, judging by the research he found on other countries that had implemented similar policies, the overall health of each country rose by twelve point five percent the first year, with greater gains the longer people received basic healthcare. It even ended up saving the countries that had implemented something similar money in the short and long term.

Why hadn't he looked into this sooner? Needing to kill time, to think about anything other than why Aurelia hadn't come back, he punched in his brother's number. It rang three times, Philip flipping through articles that showed transition schedules to cover the country and not put it into bankruptcy while he waited.

"Hello? Philip?" Philip looked down at his home screen, confused. He recognized the voice that picked up, but unless he was operating on muscle memory, he'd made a pretty big error in numbers. He hadn't dialed her number in over a year, usually only spoke to her regarding official state business.

"Marjorie? Didn't I dial my brother?"

"You did. He's speaking with the Ambassador right now and asked that I answer to make sure everything is okay since it's the middle of the night there."

No. Everything is not okay. And much of the reason it wasn't was due to the way the woman on the other line had screwed with his heart, making it near impossible for him to trust again.

"It's fine," he muttered, annoyed.

"I know you better than you think. What's going on? Is it the reporter? Did she leave?"

"Her name is Aurelia, and she's a journalist. And I don't know. Will you just have Robert call me when he's free?"

"Can I give you some advice, Philip?"

"Sure," he said, his forehead cradled in his uninjured hand. Though it was the last thing he needed at the moment, the woman who'd savagely stomped on his heart passing down her words of wisdom.

"Let her go," Marjorie told him, her voice quiet.

"What are you talking about, Marjorie?"

It'd been a while since he'd let Marjorie under his skin, but that didn't mean she didn't try.

"The woman. Aurelia. Let her go. I miss you, Philip." Her voice was barely audible, it was so soft.

Philip's chest shook with a building rage. His brother was in the same room as Marjorie, and she was doing what she did best—messing with their lives to get what she wanted. She was probably sick of the life of a queen with the travel, the dignitary events, the baby-holding and politician hand-shaking, so she was going back to what was familiar. To him.

Well, he wasn't having it. Not a freaking word of it.

"Have my brother call me, Your Grace, and be very grateful I am not going to speak a word of this to him. Good night."

He hung up the phone and went to his suite. It was pristine, immaculate, the comforter brought up, the throw pillows perfectly placed. Slowly, reticent about what he'd find, he opened the drawers on the chest next to his bed. They were empty except for the deposit check he'd given Aurelia for half the fee he'd promised.

Everything that was holding him upright dissolved. He slid to his backside, holding the small piece of paper like a lifeline that would give him answers.

Minutes passed, but nothing came to him except the staggering realization that she was gone. He stood, dizzy with fatigue.

Rest was necessary, but so was finding out what happened to Aurelia.

He ran to the kitchen to find it empty, the staff in bed, most likely. He could raise an alarm, get them all there in a matter of minutes, but that was the one perk of being royalty he'd never fully ascribed to. Besides, Aurelia hated being waited on by guards, by the staff, by him. How would she feel if she knew that in order to get her back, he'd roused the entire country?

As he made his way back to his suite, saw again how empty it was, that all evidence of her ever having been there was gone, he bit his bottom lip to avoid the heat that built behind his eyes. She'd evaporated like a ghost that would haunt him every day for the rest of his life. His only remaining question was whether or not he was willing to let that happen, or if he would go after her, put it all on the line like he'd never done before.

The war he waged with himself offered no answers. For once, he needed someone who knew him better than he knew himself. He needed his advisor.

He went to Gregory's suite and found the door cracked open, a light on inside. His good hand was poised to knock when another voice came from the other side of the door. It was a female voice, one that he recognized straight away, but the shock of finding her there, in Gregory's apartment, was jarring.

Patricia? He strained as close to the open door as he could, but only caught snippets of their conversation.

"—gone. Sometime tonight."

"Will she be—"

"—not sure. It depends on the baby."

The baby? What baby?

In less time than it took for Philip to ask Aurelia to stay the month—a memory that now seemed a million light-years in the past—he put all the pieces together. Aurelia unable to eat, her sickness that seemed to get worse each day, Patricia keeping such a close eye on Aurelia, making sure she got her rest. The way Aurelia could fall asleep in minutes even in the middle of a fight.

She's pregnant.

Philip's mouth went dry, all the moisture flooding to his palms. The tears that threatened before fell steadily now, but he hardly noticed as they spattered his shirt. His mind spun, his heart raced.

It had to be his, but then why hadn't anyone told him? All the emotions roiling inside his chest sprang to the surface, cascading over him.

Philip barged into the room, the door cracking hard against the stone wall behind it.

"Jesus," Gregory shouted, jumping to his feet. "Knock much?"

Patricia didn't seem at all surprised to see him. She simply nodded, her arms crossed over her ample bosom. If anything, she looked ready to try and hang him for his crimes. Not that he blamed her.

"So," Gregory said, walking slowly over to Philip, his hands in his pockets. Philip understood his reticence. He'd acted like a first-class jerk the last time they'd talked and hadn't been doing much better since. "How much did you hear?"

Patricia's eyes bored holes in the side of his head, but she didn't move, her arms now resting on her wide hips.

"The baby. Please tell me it's mine."

Philip heard the desperation in his voice. He was begging for things he had no business wishing for.

"Please. She's not my type. How many times do I have to tell you that?" Gregory winked and laughed.

Philip once again envied his friend the carefree lifestyle he lived, but for the first time, his jealousy dissipated as quickly as it came. He was going to be a father. He was going to have a child with a woman he was in love with before this crucial piece of information surfaced. Philip looked at Patricia, his eyes pleading and refilling with tears he had no ability to thwart.

"Is it true?"

"Well, yes, it's true, you daft boy."

"Why didn't either of you say anything?" he asked.

Gregory threw his hands up and shook his head. "Nope. I just found out. I'm off the hook for this one."

Patricia, on the other hand, stood. Philip was actually scared about what she might say. "Your Grace, you're the smartest man I know, but you do and say some of the stupidest things, Philip Anthony."

"Why? What did I do?"

"Have you told her you loved her?" Patricia's hands were now on her hips, her mouth turned down in a scowl.

"Um, no. Well, yes. When she was leaving."

"Mm-hmm. That's what I thought. And did you tell her everything she needs to know to stay?"

Philip sighed and shook his head. Had he known her secret, though… But that didn't matter to her. She needed to hear it without having to tell him about the baby. He understood. Albeit, a little late, per usual.

"No, ma'am."

"Precisely. And you think a young woman is just going to stroll into your room between bouts of losing her cookies and say, 'I'm having your baby, Philip. What might you think about that?' No, sir, that's not how we women work. She left because she didn't feel wanted, so it's up to you two numbskulls to figure out a way to change that. God help us all that you're the only hope of bringing her back."

Philip laughed, wiping at the stray tears that fell. "I'll admit to all that. But what do I do? She's gone."

"She is. But that can be fixed with a plane ride and apology if you're willin' to do both. And soon. Don't let that wee baby sit for another minute inside a momma who doesn't think the daddy wants it."

If his heart could have stopped dead and left him standing there, mouth agape, he'd swear that was what happened. He hadn't meant to let Aurelia—let alone the baby he hadn't known existed until that very minute— think he didn't want them both, but that was what he'd done, wasn't it?

Jesus. He had work to do, and not a lot of time to do it.

He hugged Patricia hard, squeezing a giggle out of the poor old woman. Snapping his fingers at the door, he gestured to Gregory.

"Let's go. You heard the woman—we've got work to do."

"Heck yes," Gregory said, whooping down the hallway.

"Been watching westerns, too?" Philip asked his friend.

"Yup. Always wanted to live the life of a rambling cowboy."

"Well, you may just get your chance. Wanna come to New York to help me win back Aurelia?"

"New York doesn't have cowboys."

"Do you want to come or not?"

"Well, duh."

Both men were smiling, Philip happy not only to have his friend back, but elated with the idea of making Aurelia his forever. He thought about the family—*his family*—that awaited him on the other end of the Atlantic Ocean, and hollered like Gregory had moments before.

With that lingering thought, and the realization he couldn't live without Aurelia, that he would do anything he could to win her back, Philip spent the rest of his restless night formulating a million-dollar plan to woo back the woman of his dreams.

CHAPTER ELEVEN: ROYAL SEARCH

The New York skyline had once been the most breathtaking view Aurelia had ever laid eyes on. The many-tiered Chrysler Building used to remind her of the drip castles she'd construct on Avalon Beach in New Jersey each summer with her family, with her mother, the harbor behind it adding to the image. The younger One World Trade Center marked New York as a beacon for all that was resilient and strong in America. Her personal favorite was the Lego-shaped New York Times building, where she spent her whole childhood wishing she could work, sharing her life-changing stories with the world.

Instead, she'd come home to an email:

Aurelia—I stuck my neck out getting you this lead. If you want to keep this contact, I need something for the paper. Anything. Let me know by the end of the week what we're publishing. Best, Nance

Now, she was storyless, jobless if she couldn't get the first part together, and altogether miserable as she sat alone in her 350-square-foot apartment, looking out over a dreary skyline that only reminded her of all the dreams she might never accomplish. It made her cry, but then, everything these days made her tear up. She would blame it on the hormones, which were somewhat responsible, but the reality was that she hated the world she'd come home to.

Her bath was barely big enough to stand up in, so how was she supposed to sit in it when she got bigger toward the end of her pregnancy? She missed the jets in the whirlpool bath in her Aldonian suite. God, how they'd help the ache in her back from her lumpy bed here.

Then there was the matter of safety. She'd never once felt unsafe in Manhattan, nor in Astoria where she lived. But now with a precious life growing inside her, all she saw were ways she could get hurt or worse. Each darkened alley, each elongated shadow was a threat. What she wouldn't give for the guards she'd lamented the existence of at each corner of the palace to be there when she got on the subway. They'd made her feel claustrophobic, sure, but at least she'd known she was safe.

If she'd stayed at her father's place in New Jersey, maybe she'd feel some iota of the comfort the people in Aldonia had given her. They'd become family, and her heart ached with the loss of their presence.

Of Patricia's kindness that was cooked into her marvelous dishes.

Of Gregory's humor.

Of Philip's hands, his lips, his sea-green eyes that drew her in like a siren's call.

So there she was, alone in an unsafe, tiny space, with no contact, one friend she was avoiding, and no boyfriend. To top it all off, she was all of those things and pregnant. Because she'd planned on staying in Aldonia the next two weeks, no one had a story for her, either. Nor would they if Nance blacklisted her for bailing on this story.

Aurelia opened her laptop, intent on doing some research and tracking down a story on her own, but her screen opened to a picture of her from behind, arms spread wide looking out over the Caucasus Range. She couldn't see her face in the picture, but she'd been smiling, at peace for the first time in a while. Since Brian, anyway.

She picked up her phone and texted Lily.

Hey girl. Home early. Meet up this week so I can fill you in? So much to dish. Xoxo

She was uncharacteristically afraid to share her recent adventures with her friend. That she'd failed in getting the story, started a no-win relationship with the Prince she was supposed to be covering, and the coup de grace—gotten pregnant. Explaining that last part was going to be more painful than a trip to the dentist and gynecologist in the same day.

Her phone dinged, indicating a response. Aurelia's finger hovered over the *open message* icon, hesitant to start going down this path with Lily. When she did, everything would be different. She'd have to come clean about everything. At least it was practice for the insurmountable task of telling her father. A surge of nausea rolled through her when she considered that Herculean task.

Unable to put it off any longer, she opened the text.

Look at you, getting the story in half the time. Hope they paid the whole $20K anyway, haha. Did you bring the royal hunk home with you? Does he have a friend? I'm still in the drought. Ugh.

Aurelia's failure welled up inside her, threatening to override the part of her that wanted to take the world by storm and write about it in the process. Lack of sex sure wasn't her problem, but everything else was.

No story, no hunk, no $$$, but lots to tell you. Miss you.

An immediate response came before Aurelia locked her phone.

Whoa. Wine at DiMarcos tomorrow night? I'm buying. Xoxo

Wine. One more thing to consider about coming home—all her social events seemed centered around alcohol, and that was most certainly off the menu for the next nine months. Even if that wasn't the case, she'd been spoiled rotten by Georgian wine and cuisine, and wasn't sure anything else would ever suffice. Damn Philip for ruining her for more than just romance; he'd single-handedly destroyed her ability to enjoy her once-simple pleasures, including a cheap glass of happy hour wine.

She groaned. How had so much changed in such a small time period? Still, if she texted anything other than an excited affirmation back, Lily would get suspicious and hound her into telling her everything over the phone. And she needed the hug that came with the gossip.

Sounds great. Six? See you then. Xoxo

Exhausted from the effort of simply existing in her old world, she sat down on her bed with the intent of only closing her eyes for a moment. Though as soon as her lids fell, she was bombarded with images of Philip and her together over the past three weeks, images that were now relegated to memories or dreams since she'd no longer be able to love him the way she wanted to.

It was close to dawn when Aurelia's eyes finally flitted back open. The start of a new day snuck under her shades, painting her bedroom pink and orange. Her stomach groaned under the injustice of subsiding only on crackers for the past day and a half, making it impossible to close her eyes and call back the images of Philip like she wanted.

She stretched, running through her stomach's list of approved foods that wouldn't come back up again in moments. Her appetite demanded a heaping portion of Patricia's dolmades, but since that wasn't going to happen, she settled on a pickle, then added a craving for an ice-cold root beer to wash it down with. She touched down on the cold floor with her bare feet, grumbling about the overall warmth she'd left behind in Aldonia.

On the way to the kitchen, something caught her attention under the door. She reached down to grab a large manila envelope, stirrings of nausea building in her chest. With the envelope in her hands, she made it to the bathroom just before bile rose from her throat.

God, please let this pass quickly.

How anyone did this multiple times in their lives was beyond her. The pain and sickness were almost too much to bear. Pickles were as obsolete a dinner choice as the dolmades were now that she'd let her hormones get the best of her. She needed to see an obstetrician now that she was home, to make sure the baby was okay. Though the idea of seeing it growing in an ultrasound without Philip there to hold her hand through the process sent another wave of nausea burning the back of her throat.

Finally, when the wave passed, she wiped her lips and opened the package she'd laid on the sink. Inside was a newspaper with a yellow sticky note attached to the top page. How very spy-like to have a secret message slid into her apartment. She smiled, recognizing the handwriting. Why hadn't Lily knocked? Aurelia hadn't seen her friend in weeks, and her chest ached thinking about how much there was to tell her best friend.

That sentiment dissipated when she read the post-it attached to the paper behind it.

You're seriously holding out on me, friend. Looks like there was a story after all. Call me, ASAP.

Aurelia's hands shook as she tore the note off to see what lay beneath it. A newspaper, and not just any one at that. It was today's edition of *The Times*. The headline turned her tremble into a whole-body shake.

What Secrets Are the Aldonian Royals Hiding? And what do the Georgians need to know before getting into bed with them?

What the...?

Oh, no. No, no, no.

Her fists balled up around the edges of the thin paper, tearing and wrinkling it. She shook, trying to contain the tremble so the rattle didn't worsen her headache. Every word of the article beneath the scathing headline shocked and enraged her. Every word of it was hers, used against her in its entirety.

Someone had crossed the line. Decimated it. But who? Who did she have to kill?

It was everything she'd lived the past month. Every last godforsaken detail. Going to Aldonia. Being asked to stay by a "member of the royal family." Living in the palace.

Her ex-husband in jail.

And God, *oh, God*, the fact that she was pregnant.

It said that she was sure her ex would steer clear of her now that she was pregnant with a royal baby.

Oh, God, oh, God.

Almost word-for-word of the first half of the article was the one she'd sent to Philip as a threat if he didn't give her something else, something to make her stay. The story she'd promised—no, *sworn*—she'd never publish was there, in print. It was all researched thoroughly, written well, but she'd never meant it to see the light of day.

Worse yet, it was complete with a photo she'd taken of him while they were at the beach house on the Black Sea. A photo that she was strictly forbidden to have taken. And yet, there it was. How? *Why?*

Oh, Jesus. This was the worst news ever. She'd never get an honest reporting job again.

For all intents and purposes, it looked like she'd written this article, this front-page, poorly-spliced half-truth.

It was her nightmare come true.

Sweet Jesus, her father would read this. He would find out about the baby at the same time as the rest of the world.

The same time as Philip.

Oh, no, oh, no.

Suddenly, the decision to leave without telling Philip about the pregnancy seemed an egregious error on her part. Fatal, even.

Sweat dappled her skin, the tremble in her hands deepening into a shiver that wracked her whole frame. Philip read the international papers every morning, *The Times* included. A glance at her watch told her she had less than an hour until he woke up, the papers waiting by his bedside to destroy the world he'd worked so hard to create.

She shoved the image of his bare torso lounging against the silky sheets, the comforter pulled up just above his waist, which she knew to be as bare as the top half of his body, out of her head. It had no place in her thoughts as they triaged what to do to save Philip, to save her, from the ramifications of this betrayal.

Without a single idea about how to fix that particular mess, she concentrated on her other problem. One just as pressing as Philip discovering her most closely-guarded secret.

She needed to contact her father.

She hadn't even called to tell him she was home yet, and now he'd read about her baby with every other early riser in New York. She was the worst daughter, the worst mother already.

She was an even worse author because she was an unwilling one.

How, *how* had someone gotten their hands on that photo?

On *her* story?

Her heartbeat against her chest sounded out a rhythm of betrayal as she scrolled through her contacts, noting how few of them there were. Lily. Her father. Gregory. A few professional sources. Loneliness set in around her like stones building a wall, closing her off to the outside world. Her support system was woefully thin. Fewer people to disappoint, though.

Before she could hit the button to call her father, her phone chimed in with another message, probably a text from Lily checking in about the article subterfuge.

Only it wasn't.

It was from Gregory.

Just seeing his name in her world sent nausea rolling in heaving waves toward her stomach, which was still empty. She regretted not eating more the night before as it rumbled but also lurched. Why would he reach out if it weren't to verbally rip into her for her story, the one she'd written, sure, but absolutely not published?

He'd probably written to warn her about Philip's wrath.

God, oh, God, what was she going to do? How could she fix this?

Unable to prolong the agony a moment longer, she swiped open his message.

Hey there, Aury. You doing okay?

That was it? No verbal lashing? Had they not yet seen the morning edition?

The nickname stung, reminded her of all she'd left behind in Aldonia. Was it really only two days ago that she was there, her lips pressed to Philip's? Since she'd joked with the effervescent Gregory? She'd left her family behind in Aldonia. More stones piled on the wall around her heart. This article had damned her from any residual hope Aldonia could ever be home.

It was never meant for someone like her, someone with nothing to offer in return.

No finesse.

No culture.

No family.

Only betrayal and horrible, horrible mistakes. She'd do better to forget she'd ever known such a place, such a man as Philip.

She sighed, resigned. *I'm fine, Greg,* she replied, including the nickname she'd given him as penance for the "Aury". *Thanks for checking in. Wish you were here for coffee.*

Decaf, she wanted to add. Instead, she typed out *How's he doing?* and sent it before she changed her mind. She got an instant reply back.

You home? Safe?

Maybe it was the grammar sensitivities that came with her day job, but the two words *home* and *safe* seemed separated on purpose. At least she could say her red-flagging system was up and running again. She tried to ignore the fact he hadn't responded to the second text, but it mocked her, sitting there with the rest of the otherwise benign conversation. Had Philip read the article? Did he hate her?

Both. Give hugs to Patricia. You, too. And tell me when you've caught up on the last season of Outlander. You'll freak.

With that, she put away her phone, her heart pounding against her chest like she'd just run the New York Marathon. She'd been prepared for everything that last night she'd spent in Aldonia—for Philip to beg her to stay, to give her all the answers she'd been searching for, anything but what he actually did. He'd gone quiet, his go-to response when she brought up anything deeper than the weather. Then, he'd let her walk out of the room, calling her bluff.

She'd threatened to leave if he didn't tell her what the hell was going on, and now she was left holding a busted hand. Her cards were shown, and the man she loved hadn't cared enough to listen to her side of the story, to see that she loved him, wanted to be with him, wanted to have his baby.

Not that any of that mattered now that it looked like she'd betrayed him, and his country, in the only way that guaranteed they'd never come back from it. Their one rule had been no photos, and she'd taken them anyway, unable to resist the pull of his figure against equally stunning scenery. She'd never meant anyone else to see it, though.

This was going to kill her or her new baby if she didn't relax. There wasn't a thing she could do about it now except wait and hope he'd listen to her semblance of an excuse.

She needed a distraction. Anything not Philip-related, not press-affiliated.

Grabbing her jacket and her purse, she decided to see if the Ample Hills Creamery might make it past the guard gate that was her overly sensitive palate. They opened early, and their rocky road was second to none—not even the gelato she'd had in Rome. Just thinking about ice cream made her stomach rumble, and Philip and the article slid further from her thoughts.

So nothing could have prepared her for opening the

door to the street to find a very confused-looking Philip holding a bouquet of lilies, her favorite flower, a suitcase beside him. He scanned the names on the wall next to the complex, his pointer finger running down the list, undoubtedly trying to find her. Only she knew without having to glance over at them that they'd long since faded, all the names and apartments victims of the harsh western sun.

"What the—" she started, unable to move from her stoop. "*Philip?*" she asked, her voice a full octave higher than normal. Of course, it was him—her heart would recognize him even if his chiseled jawline was hidden from sight—but the juxtaposition of him there, in person, two feet from her in her hometown was too much for her to process. For the umpteenth time, the tears fell, but this time, her chest heaved under the weight of missing him, and sobs wracked her body. How she'd made it across the Atlantic without him was beyond her comprehension at that moment.

He turned to her, his own eyes damp, his breath hitching in his oh-so-delectable chest. Was it possible that there, against the dull gray and machinated backdrop of New York, Philip was more handsome, more luminous than he'd been in Aldonia? He was the sun, shining down on her world, making it bright again. However, the stark relief between him and the world he represented and the one she resided in was a cruelty that tugged at Aurelia's heart.

That crushing feeling was overridden, though, by him being there did to parts of her that had been dormant since her return to the States. Moisture seeped from between her legs as she took in his tall frame, the tic in his jaw as his gaze raked over her, the way his full lips twisted into a grimace.

"I'm sorry," she spat out, keeping her distance until she could gauge how upset he was.

"For leaving? Don't be. I know why you did. That's my

fault, and it's the reason I'm here." His finger traced her jawline as it had when he'd first had her alone in her suite the night they met. It disarmed her, made her forget the glaring issues they still had to overcome.

The pregnancy.

The article.

Wait. Was it possible he didn't know?

"No, for the article. Have you seen it? Please say you haven't seen it. I didn't write it, Philip. You have to trust me." She was rambling, powerless to stop the verbal onslaught. Her body reacted of its own accord around Philip, just as it had in Aldonia.

Confusion etched his chiseled features, then realization dawned on them. A smile broke out on his lips, knocking her wall down stone by stone. He closed the fractured millimeters between them, holding out the flowers and a copy of the same paper she was trying to escape.

"I did see it, and I know you didn't write it. In fact, I've got people on it right now, Aurelia. I—" he began, but he didn't get past that before her lips were on his, her hands fisted in his hair, her tongue running over his bottom lip, tasting mint with a hint of spice. Heat flooded her system, and a groan of pleasure escaped between them.

"I guess that's my cue, then," she heard from behind her. She begrudgingly broke off from the kiss and spun to see Gregory there, a body-sized backpack slung over his shoulders. He looked remarkably at home in the city, loose-fitting jeans and a red and blue plaid flannel adding to the very American aura he gave off. He'd always wanted to visit and now he was there, in her hometown. It seemed too odd to be real.

"Gregory!" Aurelia squealed. She looked back and forth between the men, unable to quelch the waterworks. "What are you two doing here if it's not to yell at me for letting the story out. Believe me, if I find out who wrote it…"

"Get in line, sister," Gregory slipped in. "Patricia's

threatened to have them thrown in Georgian prison, a fate worse than death."

"Wait, how'd you get a copy of it so quickly?"

Philip smiled, though she noted it didn't reach his eyes, which were a light gray. Not quite the calm she'd seen at the beach house, but not a raging storm, either. She wanted to help, wanted to be there for whatever bothered him, but she wasn't sure that was her place. Not anymore. That, and she had so much to tell him, if he'd listen. So much that he needed to hear.

"We're ahead of you ten hours, not behind, remember? We got a copy before we made it to the runway last night."

"Oh, God. Then why didn't you tell me it was coming? That you were coming here? Am I in trouble? Really?"

Nerves fluttered over her skin, warming her for the first time since she'd arrived back in New York.

Gregory's gaze darted to Philip and he whistled, rocking back on his heels.

"I'll leave that to the guy with the flowers. You two enjoy each other. I'd say be good, but that doesn't sound like any fun."

As soon as Gregory was out of sight, Philip turned back to her.

"You're not in trouble, Aurelia. I should never have let you get on that plane, but even still, even as mad at me as you have a right to be, I never doubted for a moment that you didn't write it. Now, can we please let it go for now? I know you don't like to be waited on, but I have a dozen people investigating the issue, including my brother. I want to talk to you about something else, something that has nothing to do with words."

He wrapped his arms around her, nuzzled her neck with his lips.

Aurelia wished she felt guilty about the staff tirelessly working to fix a mistake she half-caused, but all she could think about were Philip's lips on hers again, the way his body felt pressed up against her swollen breasts. Not even the answers she'd left Aldonia without mattered at that moment. Her body was in charge, her only job to let it lead the way.

The rest could wait.

She gazed up at him, forgetting how small she felt in his arms, how safe. Pulling him toward her door, the lust in his eyes sparkled for her, driving her forward. Who cared that he'd let her leave, that they still had everything to talk about? All she could think was getting this man to her bed.

The hormones surging through her body seemed relieved to have a fun task to accomplish, something other than evoking tears and sobs of heartache.

Philip pushed the elevator button and wrapped his arm snugly around Aurelia's waist. His thumb rested along her panty line and he dug it deeper into her skin. She gasped but didn't move. His hand slid further down her hip so that his thumb was dangerously close to the apex where her thigh met her sex. When the elevator doors finally opened, Philip's hand disappeared to his side, leaving her skin tingling, burning where he'd touched her.

God, she wanted more, wanted *him*.

An elderly couple exited, smiling at Philip like they recognized him, their heads pulled together in whispers. He dipped his head in deference to them and dragged Aurelia inside the elevator just as the doors closed around them.

"Was that about—" she began, but then he was on her like the fate of both of them rested on how fast he could take her, how close he could bring their bodies. She responded in kind, opening up her mouth so his eager tongue could explore and taste all it wanted. When she slid her tongue along his, he pressed her up against the wall of the elevator that was moving too slow for her needs.

The elevator stopped unexpectedly and chimed, warning them the doors were opening, but a quick glance at the numbers showed they still had three excruciating floors to go before she could have her way with Philip. Again, like he was trained in the art of subtle seduction, Philip put two feet between them before a group of guys in matching flannel shirts not unlike Gregory's entered.

She just stood there, panting like an idiot. Thank God the men couldn't see what was going on beneath her clothing.

"Evenin'," one of them said, dipping an authentic-looking cowboy hat at Aurelia.

"Good evening," she responded, unable to regulate her breathing. She snuck a glance at Philip, who had sidled back next to her in the back of the elevator to give the men room. How the heck could he look so calm when every hair of hers stood on end, every cell screaming how badly she wanted this man? He appeared as if he'd recovered just fine from their steamy encounter. In fact, he was staring straight ahead like he didn't know her from Adam. It made her furious and hot at the same time, which only served to make her even more furious.

"We're from the Treasure Valley," one of them said, half-turning to Aurelia. "Bachelor party for this lucky schmuck who gets to marry my sister."

Philip's hand snuck up Aurelia's skirt, and one finger slid between the fabric of her panties and the delicate folds they hid. Holy hot heck. What was he doing? She tried to hold in her small gasp, mask it as a response to the gentleman who'd spoken. Luckily, it came off that way.

"I'm Owen. Nice to meet you," the betrothed cowboy said. He reached around to shake her hand, which took with all the strength of a mouse. When she shook his hand, Philip's finger circled within her faster, teasing her center, making her drip with pleasure. The men were too cramped in the small space to see a thing, but the illicitness of the maneuver was not lost on Aurelia. She squeezed Owen's hand so hard it hurt her own, and he grimaced.

"Pleasure," she said, meaning the word in more than one way.

"Grabbing this man's ID so he doesn't get thrown outta yet another swanky bar, and then we're on our way. You two enjoy your evenin'," the first cowboy said to Aurelia.

Aurelia had no question about how much she and Philip were going to enjoy themselves that evening, starting as soon as the elevator doors closed. As soon as they were alone again, Philip refrained from pulling her close, and instead, slipped another finger inside her, eliciting a moan of pleasure from Aurelia. She braced herself against the wall of the moving box, barely able to stand as his fingers glided expertly inside her, rocking her within an inch of an orgasm that rivaled anything they'd shared so far.

At the ding letting them know they'd arrived on Aurelia's floor, Philip scooped her up in his arms, his fingers remaining deliciously in place as he carried her to her apartment. She fumbled in her purse for her keys, and with shaking hands, barely opened the three locks on her door.

God, how she wanted this man.

Finally, after an eternity, they were behind her door, locks back in place. Philip wasted no time sitting Aurelia down, shimmying her dress over her head and tossing it to the ground. He groaned with pleasure when the move revealed she wasn't wearing a bra. He licked his lips and she longed to be the tongue that ran across his skin. Never had she felt so powerful, so captivating as when he looked her over and growled with deep appreciation.

"You, my love, are the most stunning creature I've ever seen. And these," he commented, cupping her fuller breasts with his hands, "I've missed them. They're different, but God, they're nice."

Heat pooled in her cheeks, and then a new fire lit below as he hooked his thumbs under the thin straps of her lace panties and pulled them down to her feet. He gazed up at her, his lashes long and thick—a sin as far as she was concerned, especially on a man as handsome and sexy as Philip. With a wicked smile, he buried his face where his fingers had been only moments earlier. His mouth covered her, his tongue moved inside her, and somehow, her swollen center felt different, more sensitive. Glorious. It was all she could do to not cry out in both pain and pleasure as he nibbled on her folds, sucking on the place that desired him most.

Holy crap.

Her heart racing, she fisted her hands in his hair, appreciating the intoxicating and thrilling blend of the thin tendrils snaking through her fingers at the same time Philip's tongue darted in and out of her.

If this is Heaven, don't let me wake up again.

"Up," she managed through halted breaths. "Come up and make love to me."

She giggled as Philip sprang up like a jack-in-the-box, the devilish grin still plastered to his face.

"I've learned never to say no when a woman asks you for something as wonderful as that. It would be like taunting the gods."

She laughed harder this time, but then the laugh turned into a nervous giggle as Philip shrugged out of his tight black t-shirt.

"We'll have to talk about your wardrobe here in New York. You look like my bodyguard."

"Aren't I?" he asked, winking as he unbuttoned his jeans and slid them off. As he stood there in nothing but a pair of red boxer briefs, Aurelia marveled at the sight of him. How such an incredibly gorgeous man was there, in her minuscule apartment, about to make love to her, was so surreal she didn't want to spend time analyzing it or she'd panic. "Speaking of changes that need to be made, this apartment won't do. I'm taking you back with me, missy. It's *Lifestyles of the Rich and Famous* or bust."

Though this idea filled Aurelia with the sort of comfort she'd only felt in Aldonia, she didn't want to start the talking part of their afternoon just yet.

"Let's talk shop afterward. Right now, I have plans to ride you like one of those cowboys we met might do with a steed."

A growl escaped Philip's chest. "Don't let Gregory ever hear you talk like that. Being a real-life cowboy is one of his only dreams."

She smiled, but it evaporated as she slid his boxers down and climbed on top of him, cowgirl-style. His body, what it did to her, was no laughing matter. She slid his shaft inside her until it filled every last need she had, plus many she didn't know existed. Her breath faltered as he rocked his hips, driving deeper inside her. Good Lord, this man knew how to give her everything she wanted.

"Do we—" he started, but she shook her head.

"You don't need anything," she whispered, crying out when he thrust harder than he ever had. "I want you to come inside me," she told him, and he nodded, his eyes never leaving hers.

Taking her cues from Philip, whose hands were on her hips guiding her speed and tilt, Aurelia slid deeper and deeper over his hard shaft, closer and closer to climaxing. When he tensed below her, his cerulean eyes turning a deep blue, she took that to mean he was close.

She bucked on top of him until he called out her name in breathless passion. She followed him over the edge, a wave of lust, and more importantly love, bringing her the rest of the way. He rubbed circles on her back with the pad of his thumb, his touch gentle yet firm. It was exquisite, per usual, but the fact that she was pregnant with their baby made it all the more special. She slid off into oblivion on his chest, which was already rising and falling with heavy, sleepy breaths.

She awoke later that afternoon, still curled up with Philip's arms wrapped tightly around her. His hands slid south, and she expected them to continue down until they found their way to the apex of desire, where remnants of him kept her wet. Instead, he stopped at her stomach and rubbed the same lazy circles on her skin with his thumb that he'd made on her back.

He kissed her neck, a far different level of heat than he'd applied to the area earlier. She purred, less worried about life and all its trappings now that Philip was there. They'd talk through the pregnancy and decide what to do together. It was a far more optimistic prospect than the one she'd been contemplating just hours prior.

"Is it true?" he asked her, his breath warm on her neck.

"Is what true?" she asked sleepily. She couldn't keep her eyes open nowadays.

"This," he replied, placing his palm firmly on her abdomen, then leaning down to kiss it softly. "I'm sorry I didn't figure it out while you were in Aldonia. All the signs were there—I was just too blind to put them together."

Aurelia's breath caught in her chest. Were they really doing this now? There? *Naked?*

"You knew? This whole time?" she whispered.

"Yes, and I'm over the freaking moon, but that's not why I'm here. Or at least, it's not the only reason. I was coming to get you either way, this just makes the trip even more worth it. I get the woman of my dreams and our baby."

Hearing him say the words *our baby* made Aurelia slick with desire. Was anything sexier than the man who had her heart talking about their family?

"Who told you?" she asked. This was only the start of the questions, but already the biggest weight was off her shoulders.

He knew about the baby. About the article.

And he hadn't run.

"I overheard Patricia and Gregory when I went to ask them for help in bringing you back."

"You really want me back?"

"Of course, I do. My life is rubbish without you in it. All vanilla. I need a little spice."

"Well, you're about to overdose on that, mister."

He snaked under the covers and kissed her belly with more passion this time, sending another surge of lust roaring through her. She tipped up his chin and teased his bottom lip with her teeth, pulling it into her mouth, sucking on the soft flesh. He groaned but inched back so that his mouth was on her cheek, his breath warm.

"Wait. We have to talk."

"Do you love me?" she asked, her hand on his already hard shaft.

He nodded, his chest trembling beneath her palm. She loved the power her body had over his, especially since he was so darn bossy everywhere else.

"Are you sure about the baby?"

Another nod from Philip that came with a groan as Aurelia's hand tightened around him, as her fingers teased his tip.

"Then that's all I need to know. The rest we can figure out later." With that, she straddled him, sliding his erection inside her up to its hilt, where she bucked and moved atop him, giving him the closest thing to a cowboy experience she could, her breasts bouncing with each thrust. He cupped them, bringing one at a time into his mouth, teasing her diamond-hard nipples, sending shockwaves of lust shuddering through her. She brought a finger to the area between his cock and perfect backside, rubbed it until he growled with pleasure.

She figured, what the hell, he'd come all the way to America for her, she might as well welcome the man properly.

And that was what she did for the next two hours.

When she awoke after some time, both sated and ravenous at the same time, she rolled over to find Philip looking down at her.

"I love you, Aurelia. I love that you're having my child, and that you make me, and the country a better place. I need to tell you about why I've been so closed off, so afraid to let you in."

She smiled, lost in his lust-laced lashes and full lips telling her everything she'd ever dreamed of hearing. She wanted to let go, enjoy the moment, but there was still so much they had to discuss, to overcome.

"I love you, too, Philip. So much. I have a lot to tell you, too. About my ex-husband, about my mother. But we can wait if you want to. You have so much on your plate, and it's all my fault. The pregnancy and the stupid article. I don't want to add to your stress."

He dipped his chin down to meet her lips, brushing them so softly it was as if a light fog had passed over them. She breathed in the heady, intoxicating scent of him.

"No. I want to do this now. I want to take you back with me, start a family together, but I can't until you know everything, until you are aware and can make your own decision."

Aurelia couldn't imagine anything he could tell her that would make her love him any less than with her whole heart the way she did now, but she nodded. He needed to do this for himself as much as her. She understood because she had secrets of her own to unburden herself of. She kissed him, pulling him as close as she could, desperate for him to understand how much she loved him. That she'd never leave.

His lips were like fire to her gasoline, making it almost impossible to do anything else but let herself be consumed by him. When he pulled away just enough for a thin layer of air to pass between them, her lips tingled with aching need.

"Yes, well, that's all the motivation I need."

He laughed, then grew serious as he launched into his story.

"Well, uh, the Queen was my fiancée. But I bet you figured that out already, huh?" He ran his hand through his hair, a wane smile on his lips. "We met in college, and she was everything I'd ever wanted, everything my parents had ever wanted. A wealthy family, a history free of anything resembling a scandal—it was the perfect match. I knew she loved me in her own way, but that didn't mean she was content with me, my title. One day, I found her and my brother in his suite."

Aurelia gasped. Sure, she'd worked out the general story on her own, but she hadn't considered that not only had the Queen left Philip, that she'd cheated on him in the process. It seemed an unnecessary cruelty.

"Yeah, it wasn't pretty. The worst part is that they didn't even stop when I came in the room. She took her time, then when she was finished, she walked over to me with the ring—my mother's ring—put in my hands and kissed me on the cheek. No goodbye, no explanation. She and my brother were married a month later and she was crowned Queen."

"My God," Aurelia whispered. "How did you survive that kind of betrayal? And to have to work with them both? It's unconscionable."

His laugh was dry and humorless. "I barely survived it, to be honest. I went on a bit of a drinking and debauchery bender that threatened everything. The affair, or rather my reaction to it, almost took down the country."

"Wow, I had no idea. Why?"

"Well, our economic system is so triggered by small blips in uncertainty that news like this would have tanked the stock market."

"It's similar in the U.S. Except a romantic scandal hardly tips the scales."

"People are already so wary of the monarchy in Aldonia, as you are aware, and for the reasons you have brought to my attention. Therefore, any hint of upheaval would be enough to ruin us."

"Is that why you have the *Duke of Puruse* thing? So it stabilizes the country when it gets bad news?"

He kissed her on the corner of her mouth and her the space between her legs warmed.

"Precisely. Our country is small enough that it would have ripple effects that last for decades so we buffer it by shutting down photos and any other technology that would create pandemonium or unrest."

She smiled at him. This was the most vulnerable he'd been, the most open. A swelling of love grew in her heart.

"And because no one had a photo of you…"

"Nor names," Philip added, smiling.

"Wow. I get it now. Gregory told me once when we first met that the title mattered more than anything else, and now it makes perfect sense." Aurelia laughed, happiness bubbling up from wherever it had been hiding out the past few months, years.

"You know, you could just rework the framework of the kingdom so your people didn't hate the monarchy. It would be good for them, too."

"Yeah, yeah, so you say. You make it sound so easy, Aury." He kissed the tip of her nose and ran the heel of his palm along her jaw.

"Well, how are you and the King now?"

Philip sighed and rolled over on his back.

"I'm not trying to make excuses for him, but he did what he had to do to get by. He was thirty and unmarried, and people talk, even all the way in that corner of the world."

Aurelia couldn't help the grin that stretched across her face. It felt good, having him back beside her, she couldn't deny that.

"I am so sorry, Philip, and for what you must have thought when you saw us. I can see how you worried I might leave you for Gregory, but you have to know all he's ever been is a good friend. Besides, I'm so not his type. He's looking for someone much feistier than me."

Philip let out a guffaw that echoed against the thin walls of her apartment. "You're saying you're not feisty?"

"I'd never try to argue otherwise, but I can say with absolute certainty that Gregory and I have no romantic connection. That day you saw us—" Aurelia cut herself off.

God, what he must have thought about her, and just after his brother and fiancée...

"I know what happened. You were sick, he was trying to help. I'll admit, even after I found out, it took me a bit to cool down, but I get it now. I was a fool to think either of you are capable of anything like that."

"Thank you. If I'd had any idea what you'd been through..." She shook her head, willing the memory of being pressed against Gregory's bare chest from her thoughts. "Speaking of Gregory, what's the story there, then? Why him? I mean, I actually got suspicious that first night because of how unroyal he is."

Philip let out a long breath of air and squeezed Aurelia's hands. She missed him so much it hurt. She never wanted a reason to let go of him again.

"That's a long story. Basically, when I couldn't function after Robert and Marjorie, Gregory was appointed by Robert to be the face of the crown—something we call a stand-in—until I could get my act together, start attending royal events, that sort of thing. He's my best friend and the man I trust most in the world aside from my private guard. Hell, even more than them. He is in the line of succession after I made him a Duke, and the rest is, as you Americans like to say, history. Honestly, until I met you, I wasn't sure I would ever take back the throne."

Aurelia blushed at the comment but understood completely. Before Philip, she wasn't sure she'd ever trust another man after Brian.

"But that's over now. I want you, Aurelia. You and you alone matter to me. Well, you and that little feisty one you're growing inside you." He reached over to her bed stand where his slacks were draped over the laminate and came back holding open a small, velour box.

She gasped with delight, tears falling steadily now. Damn those hormones. She didn't want anything to blur her vision of him as he slipped off the bed and knelt in front of her. As much as she'd admonished his gift-giving as being too ostentatious, he'd nailed this perfectly.

In the same shape as her mother's pendant, a three-carat diamond sat in a bed of smaller stones, all surrounded by white gold that glittered in the light. On the sides were cutouts that let the light in, just like the lamp in her room back at the palace. Well, her old room. Everything changed when Philip slipped the ring on her trembling hand.

"Aurelia," he whispered, slipping the ring on her finger as she nodded. He didn't have to ask, but she hung on his every word as he did. "Will you marry me, be my queen, and help me bring Aldonia into the twenty-first century? Starting with running its PR Department. You're damn good at it, you know."

He winked and she laughed, still nodding like a love-sick fool.

"Yes," she whispered. "Yes, I'll marry you and have a bajillion children with you and help make Aldonia the best country it can be. God, I love you, Philip," she said, wrapping her arms around him, bringing her naked chest against his, his heartbeat thumping against her chest.

Her heart outside her body.

With a single word, she'd said goodbye to her past and welcomed in her future, a future that looked as filled with love and laughter and joy as any she'd ever imagined.

He kissed her, and every fear about not being good enough, not being right for Philip's royal life evaporated as his tongue teased hers out. She was right for Philip and that was all that mattered.

EPILOGUE: THE ROYAL FAMILY

Aurelia looked at the newspaper's front page, trying not to gloat with a smile that she seemed incapable of hiding. The headline read "New Aldonia Royal Decrees Bring Country to the Head of the World Stage."

"It's great, love. I'm proud of you. This is huge for you, for us."

She nodded. She must look like a clown, bobbing her head and grinning, but she couldn't help it. It had been the most whirlwind past year. Though in the beginning of her time working as the head of PR for the royal family it was difficult to adjust to the exposure, now it fulfilled her in a way she'd always hoped journalism would.

Her first story, the one that had solidified her as the new voice of the royal family, was the one that simultaneously cleared her name. She'd followed her fiancé back to Aldonia and immediately jumped on the team in charge of investigating the intellectual property theft of her original story. Of course, Philip had been vehemently against it at the start. He'd worried about the stress, the harm that it might cause Aurelia or the baby. She'd only been able to convince him by explaining that writing was what calmed her, made her feel alive.

So, she'd used her red flags, and the clues Philip could give her about who would want to cause his administration harm, and tracked down the guilty party.

It had been Marjorie, the Queen and Philip's ex-fiancée. Aurelia hadn't been surprised, but heartbroken for her soon-to-be husband. He'd given up so much of his life— ruling his country, his confidence, his hope that love was a restorative, wonderful thing to be cherished— all for her. And then she'd decided if she couldn't have him, no one could. Somehow, she'd gained access to his cloud, the online portal that housed all his photos and documents, found the article and damning photo, and sent it in anonymously.

Of course, Robert had filed for divorce, taking their newborn daughter with him. Despite the awful, vindictive things Marjorie had done to Philip, it was her dismissal of her daughter that put her in disregard with Aurelia. She'd told Robert she never wanted to be a mother anyway and left without a fight. Aurelia couldn't imagine giving up her daughter for a moment, let alone forever.

Robert was devastated, but Philip was there for him to help take over the governing of Aldonia until his brother could get on his feet. It was then Aurelia had known her decision to marry Philip had been the best she'd ever made. He ruled wisely, empathetically, and with a look to the future of their country. He'd taken her advice, and her research had been consulted each time a major decision needed to be made with regard to their policies.

Them, she'd cover them honestly and in-depth, including talking to the constituents she and Philip represented. It was fulfilling work, and the country had flourished under her husband's governance.

She'd never been happier or more at peace.

"I agree. Your country has responded well to the changes." She pointed to the graph on the front page, showing the incline in the overall health of the citizens, the decline in medical-associated costs in the year since the plan was initiated.

He wrapped his arms around her from behind. "*Our* country. And yes, it does. Speaking of doing well, will you look at her?"

Aurelia watched their daughter toddle around the room, giggling as Gregory's new Labrador puppy lapped at her face.

"She's pretty darn perfect, isn't she?"

"With her genes, it'd be hard to imagine otherwise," Philip said, kissing his wife's cheek. When his lips migrated to her neck, Aurelia giggled not unlike her daughter. This man still had the power to make her knees weak, heat pool in her belly. How it was possible to have such a deep love for someone while at the same time wanting to tackle him and rip his clothes off, she had no idea.

But she liked it.

"Where do you think we should have her party? The gardens? My father loves them..." she trailed off, her eyes damp and wistful. "I can't believe she's already a year old. The time went by so quickly." Philip was the best father, and Aurelia's heart ached watching them together, wishing time would pass slower so she could hardwire every memory into her subconscious.

"I know just the place to take her, and your father," he said, smiling down at Aurelia.

"The beach house?"

"That's the one. Will it be okay? I mean, it's no palace garden..." he teased. Philip knew her father loved the beach house almost as much as he did. He took his granddaughter to the sand by the south end of the bay to build castles each morning, loved when she stomped them at the end of the day, squealing with joy. Having her dad in Aldonia had been the highlight of her move there. Plus, he seemed to hit it off with Patricia, which she planned to pursue more with him later.

She hit Philip on the shoulder playfully, but he caught her hand and pulled her in a for a kiss that ignited her core and set her skin ablaze.

"Wanna leave our perfect little angel with Patricia and my dad for a minute and head upstairs?" She trailed her hand along his hips, then moved it to the inside of his thigh, feeling his breath hot on her neck.

"Just a minute? Should I be offended?"

"I think I could help make it last a little longer. Are you up for an afternoon?"

"You're feisty again. I can't say I mind." His hands moved up from her waist and cupped her breasts. "It's a good thing you're not knocked up so we can get that heart rate elevated again.

"Actually, there is something I wanted to wait until the birthday party to tell you." Her cheeks flushed again, betraying her emotions. This time she didn't care. She was beyond happy and wanted him to know it.

Philip pulled back but left his hands high on Aurelia's waist. His gaze dipped to her stomach, still flat, but that wouldn't last long.

"Are you saying…?" he asked, his eyes sparkling, moisture pooling in the corners of his eyes, making them appear an even brighter green. God, she loved this man. She nodded, heat building behind her own eyes.

"I am."

"When?"

"I'm about a month along."

Philip picked her up and spun her, then set her down just as abruptly.

"Are you okay? I mean, I don't want to hurt you," he told her, his breath shaky.

She laughed. "This time is much different. You don't have to worry, according to the physicians."

"So we can still ask Patricia for the afternoon?" he asked, the twinkle in his eyes taking on a different heat.

She pulled him close, placed his hands back on her chest.

"You'd better ask her soon, mister, or our poor

daughter will be scarred by what she sees."

Philip held her cheeks in his palms and kissed her before he ran off in search of Patricia. Aurelia watched Noelle roll on the ground with the puppy, laughing. Soon, she would have a little brother or sister to play with, and Aurelia would have everything she never knew she always wanted. When hands snuck around her from behind, sliding up her shirt, she laughed, turning toward her husband.

"I love you," she said, trying to catch her breath. "I'm so happy."

"I love you more," he told her. Nudging her down the hall with his arms still wrapped around her, she recalled her first time in this hallway almost two years ago. So much had changed—her job, her family, her home—and yet she couldn't be happier. "Forever," he added.

"Forever," she said, and meant it. She didn't want to wish a moment away, but she looked forward to seeing what that looked like with Philip, with her family.

For now, though, she had her arms around her prince, and that was the only place in the world she wanted to be.

KRISTINE LYNN

SNEAK PEEK AT THE SECOND BOOK: A BRIDE FOR THE ALDONIAN KING

Chapter One: The Girl

A paralyzing scream tore through Lorelai's otherwise calm walk of the stables. Her legs erupted in goosepimples, then acted on autopilot, propelling her with a purpose beyond feeding the horses.

Someone was in her barn.

With her horses.

Another peal of terror ripped through the air, lighting a fire in her chest. The same fear she'd shoved aside since her father's heart attack—fear her world was close to teetering off course—fueled the blaze.

Adrenaline coursed through her, sending her pulse north of one-eighty. She dropped the bag of feed from her shoulder, letting it *thump* in the dirt, and took off like the Devil was at her heels. The stable staff wasn't due to arrive for another week, so whoever was in the barn definitely shouldn't be.

From the sounds of things, they'd figured that out, too.

When she whipped around the corner, she froze as she

took in the scene in front of her, too surprised to say or do anything but watch. A bubble of giddiness rose up her throat, but she choked back the laugh that could easily have turned into a sob of relief.

No one was hurt.

Just a young girl—maybe toddler was a better word—atop Lorelai's shoeing stool, stretched out on her tiptoes in scuffed black mary janes, her arm arched up and over the top of the cherry wood stall door that housed Lorelai's chestnut mare, Billie Jean. Billie Jean gave a palm-to-finger lick of the child's hand, eliciting another stomach-curdling scream followed by a fit of giggles.

Relief flooded Lorelai's system, purging out the fear that lay dormant, waiting for the opportune time to rear its ugly head again. She needed to get a handle on that, and quick. She couldn't run her own hunting operation if she was crippled by fear every third minute. And she would run her own hunting operation—she'd see to that. Otherwise what was she doing back here in a place riddled with memories that haunted her around every corner?

Speaking of things she needed to get figured out, ascertaining the identity of her secret stowaway was in order. But not just yet. The girl was having too much fun for Lorelai to jump in and spoil it too soon. She observed the child and horse together for a full three minutes, biting back a laugh each time the horse's tongue made contact with the girl, who squealed with joy. It was darn near the cutest thing Lorelai'd ever seen. It was also an all-too familiar sight, down to the tight auburn curls that fell down the back of the eager child. Lorelai's stomach lurched as she realized who the young girl reminded her of—herself.

She shut her eyes against the unrequested barrage of memories that assaulted her. The sounds of the horses as they snorted, whinnied, and chomped their food caused her heart to seize, adding to the threat of the images dancing at the back of her lids.

Her father reaching down, his brown eyes filled with love, passing off a salt lick for her to give the ponies when she wasn't much older than this girl.

His hands spanning the width of her waist as he lifted her atop her first horse, Winny.

Walking her through the pasture, describing his duties—hers now—as he squeezed her hand with excitement.

The rough working-man's skin of his hand on hers still tickled after all these years.

She let out a sigh riddled with guilt and love both.

If he were alive, he'd love this scene taking place in his old barn. Another young girl betrothing herself to the animals, to their care. Her heart threatened to beat out of her chest thinking about her father, about the barn and man who had raised her within its four walls. She cleared her throat, swallowing her past back into the pit of her chest where it belonged.

There would be time to mourn, but not yet. Not if she wanted to make a name for herself in the hunting community and get out from under the grief that washed over her like a rogue wave every time her father's face stormed her thoughts.

Forcing the issue, the girl let out a screech as she tumbled off the stool, landing on her backside, silk skirt and tulle petticoat up around her waist. Lorelai rushed to her side just as a solitary tear slipped down the girl's cheek, Lorelai's memories of her father all but forgotten for now.

"I'm okay," the girl huffed, standing up and brushing the red dirt from her dress with one hand, swiping at the tear with the other. She was all defiance and sass wrapped in the most precious package Lorelai'd ever seen. In that way she and the girl were different as night and day. She hadn't worn dress shoes outside of the Christmas pageant her father dragged her and Gregory to each year and not since, either.

No, she was a stable girl, through and through—no

time or energy for frills in her life.

**GET YOUR OWN COPY….
AVAILABLE WHERE BOOKS ARE SOLD…**

ACKNOWLEDGEMENTS

This book would not have been possible without the love and support of my family and friends. For a woman with a penchant for happily-ever-afters, I feel like I won the lottery with you all. You make every day better.

To my mom and dad, thank you for keeping me on track, for offering to read drafts, and for being the first to buy my books even though you've read them already.

To my husband and daughter, thank you for the gift of time and space to write about fake people in fake worlds and for reminding me to take breaks and enjoy the world I share with you both.

To my writing partners, Anna and Kate, who champion my work and are always willing to talk about books and characters and everything romance. You two are the best, and I can't wait to see your books on shelves.

To Stacy and Erica, who have been on this romance kick with me since the start. Colleagues come and go, but friends like you two are as forever as fairytale romances.

Finally, to my readers, thank you. Taking a risk on a book and an author is a leap of faith and I hope I've done you proud. You're the reason I love what I do, the proof that love really does make the world go 'round.

KRISTINE LYNN

www.ingramcontent.com/pod-product-compliance
Lightning Source LLC
Chambersburg PA
CBHW030547200626
46812CB00022BA/2645

ABOUT THE AUTHOR

Kristine Lynn is the author of the *Treasure Valley* and *Secret Prince* romance series, as well as the linked collection of short stories, *Shrapnel.* When she's not writing, she's teaching college students in Arizona and enjoying the Southwest with her husband, daughter, puppy, and three-quarters of a desert tortoise. To connect with Kristine (who also writes under Kama O'Connor), you can email her at kristinelynnauthor@gmail.com or follow her on social media.

Twitter: @kristinelauthor
Facebook: @kristinelynnauthor
Goodreads:
https://www.goodreads.com/user/show/19811168-kama-o-connor
Website:
https://kristinelynn.wixsite.com/author/about

KRISTINE LYNN